—She was gifted with a profound shrewdness and entered upon womanhood in quite a wonderful way. She flirted with her tutor and enraged him so that he showed less reserve and authorised more frequent nocturnal visits.

The consequence was an exhaustion and a weariness in the child which troubled the family, without their suspecting for a moment what was the cause of her ill health, so she was sent into the country to her grandmother to recruit her strength.

Being thus warned, the priest observed much more reserve after her return, and finding that she could not gratify her desires in the way she had hoped, with her tutor, Adelina turned to her brother for help.—

GREEN GIRLS

GREEN GIRLS

ANONYMOUS

Translated from the French

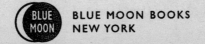

BLUE MOON BOOKS
NEW YORK

Published by
Blue Moon Books
841 Broadway, Fourth Floor
New York, NY 10003

Copyright © 1988 Blue Moon Books, Inc.

ISBN 1-56201-144-8

Manufactured in the United States of America

Book One

Chapter One
Leaving for School

I

Profound silence pervaded the house of Mirzan, at Chartres, and nothing betrayed the discovery of the sad adventure, which had happened within its walls.

No loud sound of voices revealed the explosion of anger which emanated from Mr. Francis Mirzan when, called by his wife, he surprised his two children, Paul and Adelina, in the very act of libertinism.

Then came a severe flogging on the backs of the two criminals, who were afterwards shut up in their respective rooms; a torrent of words, among which some epithets like

1

scamps, culprits, wicked children destined to dishonour their parents etc.; and then the calm; the mother's tears; the father's reflection; the decision to send them as boarders, one to a college and the other to a convent.

Mr. Francis Mirzan, a magistrate of the old school, was austerity itself, and Mrs. Isabelle Mirzan was of the most devout principles.

Paul Mirzan, who was thirteen years of age, received the paternal correction with rage and fury; Adelina Mirzan, a girl of fourteen, the more guilty of the two in the affair, received it with icy and haughty impassibility.

The children had been brought up at home. A clergyman gave them their lessons; and as no previous signs had announced the depraved instincts of the children the incident came like lightning from a blue sky, and yet there were links connecting the event with the past.

Ever since her first Communion, celebrated when she was twelve years old, Adelina, who was of a precocious and vivacious nature, showed signs of a sudden inquisitiveness, which inflamed her blood and made her understand at an early period what is generally concealed from children.

She was tall for her age, slender, with fine limbs, a pretty, fair-complexioned girl, with innocent eyes, which hid from ordinary observers her true mental excitement, and lustful thoughts.

The priest charged with the instruction and education of the two children was a middle-aged man, possessing every qualification necessary to accomplish the task confided to his care.

He was, however, ugly, stunted, and almost deformed, and was pitted with small-pox; and he had led a rather laborious life and his gratitude and strict moral principles guaranteed his reliability to the Mirzans.

How did it happen that this man, this saint, conjectured

and at once understood the sensual agitation of the little Adelina and felt the effect of it himself?

With regard to the management of the children he enjoyed the most complete freedom and confidence, and commenced his pleasant last secret task by detaining the girl now and then after school under pretext of explaining the more difficult part of her lessons or of helping her to work out a somewhat abstruse problem, and then, in the solitude of the school room, when their chairs were drawn close together, their eyes fixed on the books, the priest's leg, while swinging to and fro, would meet Adelina's leg, which was never withdrawn on such occasions.

Their hands met also, and all the while he was teaching or pretending to teach, Abbé Dussal kept the fingers of his little companion in his firm grasp, conveying to them by the force of his own feelings a strange fire, which made her blush and in which she delighted.

These were the preliminaries of love!

The child, accustomed to the priest's ugliness, felt that the hour had come when he would reveal what she burned to know and she encouraged him to the best of her knowledge, and only the fear of a scandal, in case he did not succeed, or was surprised, checked his ardour.

When Adelina entered on her fourteenth year her figure was rather lean, but very promising. And as a bitch in heat her whole body showed the strong desires of her flesh. There were on both sides gropings with hands, legs, and these bore the similitude of voluptuousness by the fact that they were both conscious of what would follow.

Adelina studied hard in order to give her teacher the opportunity of protracting the school hour and her family was amazed at her progress and desire of learning.

No suspicion troubled their minds, and the priest was therefore free to make his first attack when so inclined.

Thus, one day, when Adelina was bending over her book, he drew the hand he held in his to his lips and sucked her little finger with so much assiduity, that she shut her eyes and threw herself backwards.

He started, let go her hand, and, turning to interrogate her, saw her moving her fingers convulsively on her dress, between her thighs.

Again their hands met and opening her eyes Adelina smiled, while she intertwined her fingers with his and squeezed them between her thighs so that her skirt, the short skirt of a child, was lifted up above her knees.

He hesitated for a moment and for the last time, casting a sly glance around him, and then, throwing back her skirt, he slipped his hand between her drawers and directed it towards her quim.

Oh, how swiftly she spread her thighs, between which appeared but a few silky curls; how easy she made it for him and how she enjoyed this touch of a man on her sexual parts! She encouraged in the most delicious manner his investigations of the little thing that tickled so delightfully and thrilled her childish body through and through.

This lasted but one minute though it seemed to be a century of bliss to both the lovers, and beneath his cassock the priest involuntarily shot out a most copious dose of sperm from his throbbing cock.

They then resumed their seats and continued the lesson without saying a word of what had happened, but the ice was broken and henceforth they had only to extend and perfect the system of voluptuousness of which they had enjoyed the first taste!

Neither one nor the other slept that night, and Adelina had to stay in bed all the next day, too exhausted with fatigue to get up. As for the priest, he walked upon thorns, supposing anybody happened to suspect the cause of this indisposition! What then?

He now fixed all his attention upon the boy, who was less fond of learning than his sister, but as soon as he was again alone with the young girl on the second day, they exchanged the same loving glances which showed them that their thoughts and feelings led them each in the same direction and only required mutual encouragement to bring about a happy termination.

He first made her stand upright before the table, as if to recite a lesson; and then he slowly slipped his hand under her petticoats and arrived from behind at her buttocks, two pretty twins, glowing with an uncommon fire.

He manipulated them tenderly, then ventured to slide his fingers between her thighs, which gently opened, as he ascended in front towards her bulging belly and frigged her cunt. He admired the presence of mind of the child as she bent over the table and fixed her eyes on the open copy-book, not to read, but to facilitate his hand-play.

Then she leaned on her elbows, rounding the lower part of her loins; he tucked up her petticoats, opened her drawers, and, not denying himself a careful inspection, contemplated with enraptured eyes the whiteness of her bottom.

They both drew a deep sigh and hastily resumed their seats for they seemed to hear the noise of foot-steps.

After the noise had subsided they studied for another minute; then the priest drew Adelina to his breast and kissed her lips for the first time.

The girl wanted very much to continue the sport, so she returned the caress very skillfully, stooped a little more forward when she saw the priest tuck up his cassock, and gently fingered the hairy monster he presented to her.

At the contact of her little hand, and its soft pressure, his cockey swelled up and poured out its liquid, and Adelina spent at the same time.

Their excitement was so great that their arms were discharged at the first contact and all traces of their final rapture (brought about but too quickly) were as well as possible removed.

The child dared not ask a single question, or make any remark as to the strange thing that had happened.

II

They had now come to a perfect understanding and observed a great deal of circumspection, often adjourning for a long time their diversions with one another.

Adelina now only awaited the first attack and the priest, relieved by his abundant and rapid discharge, enjoyed his felicity and studied the means of increasing the opportunities and extending the field of action.

Seeing them so perfectly quiet without the least change of attitude, it was impossible to suspect the licentious thoughts which passed through their brains.

For more than a week they did not remain alone together after school, for the priest could not neglect Paul and constantly occupy himself with his sister.

Adelina's heart throbbed violently when the door was shut for their next *tête-à-tête*, and she stood watching every motion of her tutor.

Under the table he approached his hand to her knee, gathered up her petticoats and began to feel her thighs. He found them well spread.

He first toyed with her skillfully and then frigged her, and she turned towards him so that he might be quite at his ease.

As he did this his hand trembled with fever; his thick lips wanted to enjoy the bloom of her youthful charms but he did not know how to set about it without making a noise, and feared such an incident would betray his greatest secret and hers also.

He had now ceased his titillations, and as on the former occasion he placed her standing before him, but this time with her back towards the table; then he made her gather up her petticoats and, stooping, touched her quim two or three times with his tongue.

"Oh, dear me, what are you doing!" murmured the girl, almost fainting.

He stopped. The blood mounted into his head and it seemed as if he would have an attack of apoplexy, but Adelina still kept up her petticoats and all of a sudden he opened his cassock, approached, and his prick entered straight between her thighs.

She shivered, her teeth chattered, and with her free hand she took hold of the knob that caressed her so deliciously.

Madness threatened to lead them further than they intended; stretching herself backwards Adelina swept all the books on the floor. They instantly resumed their usual attitude. Picking up the books the priest commenced some scientific explanation connected with her lessons, but as nobody disturbed them, they again embraced and kissed one another.

After a time the priest rose and audaciously put his prick to the lips of his pupil.

At first she did not understand what he solicited and only kissed it timidly; but he pushed on and separating her teeth introduced it into her mouth.

It was but part of a caress. They could not allow themselves the luxury of intoxication.

They parted and resumed their work, exchanging still some caresses with their lips, but as soon as their senses began to stray, they rapidly suspended the voluptuousness.

Both felt their thighs getting wet without experiencing the thrilling sensation of other joys.

They wanted so much and feared everything, discovery above all things, and they were compelled to part without having satisfied the craving of their senses.

The priest did not sleep a wink that night.

He occupied a room at the end of a passage, near which was the water closet. Adelina had her room beside that of her mother; but the latter would not wake even at the detonation of a cannon.

At one o'clock in the morning the girl was still tossing herself restlessly in her bed; then she rose cautiously, slipped on a petticoat and her slippers, and softly left the room.

She went straight to the priest's door. Had he a presentiment of the adventure or did he try to magnetize her at a distance? The half-open door showed her that she was expected.

She entered without hesitation, and feeling her way, guided by the priest's breathing, approached his bed; stretching her arms before her she met his hand; he pushed her head toward his thighs, between which his cockey was raised to a haughty pinnacle.

Oh, she would have paid for that minute by copying twenty thousand lines!

She took his prick into her mouth and swallowed it up several times, while he tucked up her petticoat, titillated her buttocks and quim, and forced his little finger into her

8

bumhole, which was all of a twitter with voluptuousness at his movements.

At times she stopped, leaned her cheek against the happy fellow's thigh, kept his prick in her hand, and patted her face with it.

Directing his hands toward her bosom the priest discovered the beginning of two darling bubbies, throbbing under his touch.

He seized his prick and raised it again to her lips, which opened gluttonously, and then he frigged it in order to spend more quickly in her pretty childish mouth.

Did she guess this? At any rate, she gave him a sudden push and retired below his knees; he had to sit up in order to catch her again.

Once he even jumped out of bed; the child had disappeared, and looking for her, he found her quite naked, rid both of her petticoat and her shift, at the foot of the bed.

He threw his arms around her, enclosed her between his legs and thrust in his prick between her buttocks.

Pressing herself against his belly, she murmured: "It is too much; oh, how delicious!"

Her childish body gave way under his weight, as he shot a torrent of thick sperm along the furrow of her bottom.

He cleaned her with his handkerchief, recommended her to be silent, to wash herself well, and then sent her away, though she would willingly have begun the pleasures all over again.

III

The priest was a prudent man. When the child was gone, he considered the danger to which he exposed himself, if she made a habit of those nightly escapades.

He trembled at the possible consequence of a surprise, to say nothing that Adelina's health might suffer seriously by this game.

Then he presented to himself the hypothesis of a possible cold, caught by moving half-naked in the passages, and he became almost mad with fear.

And retaining her the next day after lessons, he therefore displayed his magisterial mien, chilling her feline temptations and encouraged her in nothing improper.

When he was about to leave her, he said: "You committed an imprudence last night. Don't begin again without my permission; otherwise I shall be obliged to suspend our little amusements."

She took his hand, kissed it and replied beseechingly: "Don't be angry; I thought of our great pleasure. It was so delicious! You'll forgive me?"

"Yes, yes, but we must avoid committing these follies. You are a clever little girl; remember that to preserve our happiness, we must conceal it from every living soul."

"You may be assured, sir, that I'll die rather than betray our secret."

Like most men the priest possessed a great deal of personal restraint. His restricted powers compelled him to check his desires from time to time, and this was fortunate for the health of the girl, who thus had to suppress her desires for some time.

Meanwhile her hot temper was aroused and her form became firm and round, and she got monthly courses at the age of thirteen years and six months. But the priest got

10

warm again and the caresses during the school time did not now satisfy him any longer.

A few months after the first adventure, it was he who asked for a second meeting.

Adelina frigged him, sucked him, and let him titillate her cunt and bubbies; he dreamt of bottom-fucking her in order to get into her soft childish body without running the risk of getting her with child.

He said: "If you can be very careful to make no noise my door will open tonight and I shall expect you."

With a misty look, she replied: "Oh yes, I'll take care, nobody shall surprise us. If necessary I shall hide under your bed and nobody will think of looking there for me!"

She was promising, Miss Mirzan!

In his own room the priest inspected minutely his mattresses and ascertained that nothing creaked and thus risked to denounce him on account of his violent movements, and when assured of the silence of these dangerous witnesses he went to bed stark naked.

At the same hour as before Adelina arrived. No noise by the opening of the door announced the entrance of the little girl, but he heard a light rustling on the carpet and was sensible of an approaching and half-smothered breathing.

He held out his hand and soon got hold of Adelina's arm, which she extended before her to feel her way.

He drew her to his breast and swiftly directed his hand to her bosom to caress her breasts.

The little things had developed; it was a delight for him to feel them, he approached his lips to suck them and the impudent wench undid her shift and let it fall to her feet with her petticoat.

At the same time she bent over the priest to facilitate his suckings and her hand wandered all over his body, shivering at the contact of these masculine nudities.

Green Girls

Interrupting her little voyage of discovery, he seized her head and glued his lips to hers.

Their sighs were mingled together, their lips were inseparably united and their tongues thrust in and and out of their respective mouths.

Ecstasy took possession of their senses as she thus enjoyed the first unrestrained caresses.

She tore herself from the delight of this voluptuousness to suck his prick, while she left her arse to the priest's manipulations.

He restrained none of his passionate desires.

Having caressed her dorsal spine he began to feel her buttocks, which, contracting under his touch, and then projecting forward, incited him to take a thousand liberties with the child. He thrust his middle finger between her buttocks and introduced it softly into the bumhole to prepare it for the act he had planned.

Adelina wriggled her back from time to time to suspend the action because of the sudden pain it gave her, but she immediately resumed her position, fearing that she had offended him, and she engulfed the whole of his prick in her mouth.

She pushed her tongue under his balls, with the smartness of a debauchee, and raised them by intermittent shoves, quickening her actions more and more.

He had got in about the half of his middle finger, and, opening her thighs, began to frig her cunt with his thumb.

Seeing that she had become accustomed to the thing, he stopped, and bringing his lips to hers, kissed them, sucking in the driplets of his own sperm, with which they were already moistened.

He drew his arms around her and lifted her gently to his side; and tossing on the bed, she cuddled to his breast.

Priapus throbbed violently against her belly. He pushed her gently away, sat up and placing her on his thighs,

12

whispered: "Do you want us to be made quite happy?"

"Oh, yes! How?"

"Turn your back to me and I'll put it into your bottom. Thus we won't run the risk of making a baby in you and can nevertheless enjoy one another as lovers."

"Oh, I'll like that!"

"You won't scream, if you suffer pain in the beginning?"

"I'll put a handkerchief into my mouth, and I'll bite on it to stifle my screams."

Children very soon make rapid progress in lasciviousness, and so do, for the matter of that, grown-up people also.

Sitting on the bed, one pressed against the other, kissing, caressing, and fondling one another, they sighed and with great difficulty made up their mind to part in order to hurry on the end of the sweet encounter.

She knew perfectly well that she would have to retire as soon as they had discharged, and she wanted to amuse herself.

On his part the priest put off the last moment in order that he might enjoy everything his fancy could suggest and that he might feel no regret if an opportunity of meeting did not present itself again.

He lifted her up, brought her arse over his face and devouring it with his tongue, spat on the orifice to facilitate his further proceedings.

His hands pressed her thighs and stretching back her arms, Adelina caressed his head, while she moved up and down, in order that she might be well licked everywhere.

With her foot she touched his cock and frigged it very skillfully.

Feeling that it was coming to a stand, he laid her down on the bed and gently directed his prick toward the orifice she presented to him. She did not stir any more than a lifeless body.

He hesitated, thrust in his finger once more, and then

applied his knob, in the bottom of his heart dreading some unforeseen event which might interrupt his lustful proceedings.

With a brisk movement of her hands she spread her buttocks, and widening her bumhole with her fingers, his nut slipped in. She started, but prevented him from drawing back.

He pushed on, the knob entered. She twitched her bottom and bent forward; he hurried on his attack: the knob had opened the way, his prick got in and their movements became delightfully simultaneous and rhythmic.

She did not fall when the crisis came; she spent at the same time that he did, pressing him to her back with both her hands.

For a minute they remained glued to one another; then he drew his prick out of the burning oven and declared the interview at an end; he advised her to pass by the water closet as if she had just taken a clyster, in order to get rid of every trace of what had happened.

"Don't forget to clean yourself well before leaving the closet," said he.

"Never fear," replied the child assuringly. "I understand pretty well that nothing must appear to show what has happened!"

Adelina was indeed a smart child for fourteen years!

IV

It became impossible for little Adelina to check her passions. She grew so hot-tempered that her manners could not but embarrass the priest.

But she was gifted with a profound shrewdness and entered upon womanhood in quite a wonderful way.

She flirted with her tutor and enraged him so that he showed less reserve and authorised more frequent nocturnal visits.

The consequence was an exhaustion and a weariness in the child which troubled the family, without their suspecting for a moment what was the cause of her ill health, so she was sent into the country to her grandmother to recruit her strength.

Being thus warned, the priest observed much more reserve after her return, and finding that she could not gratify her desires in the way she had hoped, with her tutor, Adelina turned to her brother for help.

Paul Mirzan, less advanced than his sister, was then in his thirteenth year. He amused himself with childish games, did not mix with boys of his own age, and lived in complete innocence of all sensual desires.

He was no fool, however; but naughty thoughts had not yet traversed his brain.

The children enjoyed great liberty, because they were thought to be possessed of religious principles and during their recreations they played together in the garden without the least surveillance.

One afternoon, when Adelina was sitting on a garden seat, seemingly reading a story, but with her thoughts wandering elsewhere, her eyes fell upon her brother who at some distance was hollowing out a reed to see if he could make a whistle of it.

She was struck with his graceful figure and thought it would be fun to initiate him into the famous, the forbidden, science to which she was so much devoted.

How could she do it? Not by any circuitous route, but by going direct to the point at which she aimed.

She made a few steps, hid behind some trees and loosened her drawers. Then, calling her brother, she said: "Paul, my drawers have come unbuttoned. I cannot arrange them behind for myself, come and help me!"

Tucking up her clothes, she presented the lower part of her body to the boy, concealed, it is true, by her shift, but betraying a respectable roundness by the way in which she moved her arse.

He stooped to pick up her drawers which lay at the feet of the foolish girl, and bending, looked under her shift.

A light seemed to dawn upon him, he lifted slowly her drawers, got perplexed, and without exactly knowing why, touched his sister's bare arse with his hand.

"Oh, Paul!" she said, with childish simplicity.

But she had raised her shift; her bottom appeared quite naked and Paul did not content himself with touching it, but rubbed it all over with great delight.

"Why, what are you doing?" said she.

"Oh, I like to feel your arse."

"How stupid of you! Why do you like it?"

"I don't know, dear."

"You have got one too, have you not?"

"Yes, but it is not so pretty."

"Let me see!"

"But if anyone should see us, Adelina!"

Adelina did not care a pin. She unbuttoned her brother's trousers, set free his little prick and feigning surprise, cried: "Oh, but what have you got there?"

"Why," said he in his turn, "how is it that you have not one like it?"

"It is however a very pretty little thing!"

"Your hands tickle it and give it pleasure."

"Caress me as I am caressing you. Oh, that's nice!"

A cracking noise of footsteps recalled them suddenly to

prudence; for they were on the point of committing a folly.

They quickly put their clothes in order again and pretended the most perfect innocence, when the cook passed to fetch some salad from the further end of the garden.

They seemed to study the plants, and the maid took no notice of them.

Having picked the salad she passed again, smiled at them and re-entered the house.

As soon as she had disappeared Paul asked his sister: "Have you put on your drawers?"

"Yes, but that does not matter; look, they are open between the legs and you can get your hand in."

"How kind you are. Let us amuse ourselves again, will you?"

"We should be better elsewhere, but they might suspect something if we returned immediately to the house. We must agree upon another time. Why, what are you doing Paul? It is not your nose that you have to thrust in there; I think it would be far nicer if you tried to push in the little thing which you have between your thighs."

Kneeling under her petticoats, Paul first honoured Adelina's front side with a short visit, and then, passing behind her, twisted her buttocks like a connoisseur, in his ingenuousness pushing his nose between them, and caressing them with his forehead, while he manipulated them with increasing emotion.

She rubbed herself against his face with great delight and they both grew more and more excited.

As he got out from under her petticoats to breathe, she made him rise, and taking possession of his standing prick, she sucked it.

They understood that if they were not to expose themselves to considerable risk of discovery they had better not prolong the game any further; they, therefore, left the thicket in which they had taken shelter.

"We will do that often," said Paul.

"Yes," replied Adelina, "but not without hiding ourselves well."

Did the priest scent the rivalry of the young brat? However that may be, he took care to inform the girl that he would expect her on the following night.

These nocturnal visits had become less and less frequent. They were only repeated at long intervals, and since Adelina's return from the country he had scarcely permitted five encounters.

When his flesh tormented him, he contented himself with titillations and spendings during school hours, and avoided running the risk of unforeseen consequences by nightly visits.

On the other hand the little girl's impudence made a great impression upon him and frightened him very much.

He only bottom-fucked her twice, restraining himself for fear of making the hole too large, which might denounce him in case of illness.

Even the most lascivious persons calculate in this careful manner.

During these escapades Adelina's impudence developed her boldness and audacity.

One night it amused her to make the priest sigh.

On entering his room, she revealed her presence by hitting lightly against a chair, and then remained quite motionless. Having got accustomed to the darkness, she saw the priest sitting up in his bed, quite perplexed, because his short-sightedness prevented him from seeing her.

One of his legs was hanging over the edge of the bed, and he stretched out his arms to seize her; he dared not move for fear of doing so blunderingly and making a noise.

She stripped off her shift and petticoats behind a chair and then came quite naked to the foot of his bed.

When the priest saw her shadow and, as she did not move, he got up and approached her. Catching hold of her childish form he hugged her in his arms and she offered no resistance to his embrace.

While titillating her fervently, he squatted upon the floor and devouring her with *minettes* and *feuilles de rose*, began to play the physician to her bumhole.

She resisted, and embracing her, he then kissed her navel, waist and breasts, pressing her closer and closer to him.

The little minx pulled his shirt towards his neck, thus showing that she wanted him to be stark naked.

He obeyed her eagerly, and leaning against his shoulder, she resigned her lips to his suckings, inflaming him so much that he tried to force his finger into her cunt.

She clasped her thighs together and rolled on the carpet beside him.

Kneeling on all fours he tongued her bumhole and then, jumping upon her arse, he bottom-fucked her in the most brutish manner, after which he went to bed, and she retired.

V

She accomplished her ablutions in the cabinet before returning to her room, and as she opened the door to get out, she found herself face to face with Paul, who with a candle in his hand, was about to enter.

Being a quick-witted girl, she did not leave him time to recover from his surprise, but blew out the light and whispered: "Are you very much pressed?"

"No, I could not sleep and made a pretext of it to get out of bed."

"If so, come with me to my room. Mamma is asleep and will not suspect anything."

The carpet deadened the noise of their foot-steps, and as a good, well-bred boy, Paul obeyed his elder sister.

She made him strip stark naked, as she had done herself, laid him on the floor and squatted over him so as to please him, then she gradually stretched herself, and the two innocents discovered the delectable attitude of love.

Adelina's bottom still retained the aromatic savour of the priest's discharge and this excited Paul very much, so that his prick increased in size and assumed quite formidable proportions.

At the sight of that, the girl interrupted her sucking, approached her lips to Paul's ear and whispered: "Bury it in my bumhole and you will be very, very happy."

Ignorant as he was of the thing he was about to do through her excellent advice, he slipped his prick into the furrow, from which it easily arrived at her bumhole.

Being still hot after the priest's assault it burned with satisfaction at this new visit; it was easy for the girl to support Paul's attack.

They kneaded one another's flesh with their fists, exchanging hot and loving kisses over her shoulder, but they did not prolong their pleasure, for the little Paul soon lost his virginity in his sister's bottom hole.

He discharged abruptly and it was only with great difficulty that he suffocated a loud cry of delight as he spent.

Content with her night's work, Adelina overwhelmed him with caresses and recommended him to go to sleep, if he ever wanted to come again. He left her; and Mrs. Mirzan had not interrupted her sleep for a minute, but continued to snore like a "grampus."

The best means to prolong these enjoyments consist in not pushing them to excess, but to preserve oneself from the dangers which always follow excess.

Being a staid man, wise and of a serious character, the priest screened himself by his infinite precautions, but the two children, who wanted experience, did not imitate him.

Those who have tasted the fruit of love once want it again and again.

Paul longed for it, and, as there was nothing Adelina liked better, she never refused to gratify his desires.

Under the thousands of circumstances which occur in daily life, they found a pretext for pleasure, an opportunity of exciting themselves; and the secrecy which they maintained before their parents and their teacher stirred the fire of their passions.

A stolen look, a sign, a touch or pressure of the hand, and they devoured with their eyes the clothes that concealed their sexual parts.

They could not always isolate themselves in the garden, and they dared not recommence the nightly scene, for on returning to his room Paul had been on the point of being surprised by his father, who went downstairs to appease an untimely hunger, which prevented him from sleeping.

They profited by a minute, by a second; she put her hand into his trousers and he directed his toward her thighs; in default of a better place they met by appointment in the water closet where they hurriedly licked and sucked one another.

At last they found a little nook in the garret, where there were some mattresses in a corner, and they agreed to meet there from time to time after school hours, going upstairs one after the other to avoid suspicion.

This went off pretty well once, twice; but the third time Mrs. Mirzan had seen her daughter climb upstairs in a mysterious manner, and she was astonished to see Paul soon follow his sister, observing the same degree of precautions which Adelina had exercised.

Their mother was puzzled for a minute and asked herself what she should do.

Guided by a strong presentiment, she went upstairs and found that the children had shut themselves up in the little nook; she looked through the key-hole and was greatly disconcerted when she saw Adelina lying on her back, her clothes tucked well up, and Paul passionately licking her little cunt.

Overwhelmed by this sight, Mrs. Mirzan had but one thought: to go and call her husband.

Before she had explained herself he understood that something serious had happened; she motioned him to follow her and both arrived in the garret as Master Paul, his prick in the air, was going to place himself in the attitude of 69 with his pretty little sister.

Their father's fury was terrible.

He broke a stick on the backs of the two culprits, who quickly tumbled downstairs before him, but they did not escape a severe lecture and flogging.

Their mother cried as if her heart would break, while their father, being by this time furious, loaded the children with abuse in the rudest terms.

They were shut up in their respective rooms, and for two days got nothing to eat but dry bread and water.

During a whole week, nobody spoke to them; but still they continued their lessons with the priest, while the outfits necessary for the establishments in which their educations were to be carried on were prepared.

Their teacher observed the greatest reserve and left the children as soon as school was over, not feeling the least remorse.

Adelina tried in vain to touch him by some stolen looks; he seemed dead to all feelings, and he trembled for fear that the tempest should reach him also.

Paul went away first with his father, who confided him to the care of the Jesuits in London.

When the mother consulted the priest about Adelina, he advised her to send the girl to the Misses Géraud's boarding school at Paris, which was especially renowned for restraining precocious passions in children.

Having obtained the best informations as to their rigour and austerity, Mr. Mirzan stopped in Paris on his way home to speak to these ladies.

He was enchanted with their kind reception, their sympathetic compassion when he made his sad confession, and this so much the more as one could not even dream of more charming and bewitching persons.

There was fortunately a vacancy in their boarding school. The Misses Géraud received only a limited number of young ladies and little girls, so, to be accepted, it was necessary to await the departure of another pupil, and the admittances were in great request.

In her turn, Adelina, whom both father and mother refused to embrace, left the house at Chartres and went to experience hew new life at school.

At first it gave her a bitter pang, but she soon got accustomed to her new surroundings.

Chapter Two
The Flagellation

I
From Adelina to Paul

I keep my promise, my dear, and write you all my thoughts as well as all my adventures. This is to comfort ourselves for all the wickedness they have shown us. You are far away, but sooner or later my letters will reach you, and prove to you that I don't care a pin for all their severity, and that I shall recommence our little pleasures whenever and as much as you like. I have cried a good deal at your departure and also when they led me away. The Abbé has not been kind; he has done nothing to defend me, and yet he ought to do so, for, I'll confess it now, it was he who instructed me in all the nice things which I afterwards taught you. Yes, my dear Paul, our so severe and stern teacher took it at his ease, when he kept me after school to caress me and make me caress him. He received me in his room at night, and he taught me that the pretty thing which the men have between their thighs is put into the woman's bumhole. Yes, indeed, he might have intervened at least for me. Now, however, I am content as it is. It was he who indicated the boarding school in which I am shut up, but I am pretty well here. For that I must be obliged to him.

After the first words spoken by Miss Juliette Géraud when we were alone, I understood that our parents have had a very happy idea, when they sent me to this house!

"Miss Adelina," said she, "we are not ignorant of the cause to which we are indebted for the pleasure of counting you among our pupils. Our system of education differs in an important degree from that which is carried out everywhere else, and if you will be reasonable, I have the firm hope that you will not repent of your sojourn at our establishment. Generally, the pupils who enter our school have committed faults like yours. We correct them in the eyes of the world by a quite benevolent proceeding. To be sure of the success we demand the most absolute silence as to the management of our school. If you comply with this rule, we shall effect the reconciliation between you and your family and we shall present to you a handsome and kind husband when your education is completed. Will you promise me this discretion?"

I must tell you that Miss Juliette is a handsome woman of thirty; a charming brunette with very delicate complexion, bewitching eyes, and a divine figure and that she does not at all remind one of the ogress I had imagined.

She continued: "You are intelligent, my child; we do not

doubt but your good intentions concerning your instruction and your conduct will reward us for all that we shall do for you. I must tell you that the system of punishment employed in our house, a system which is prohibited in France, is flagellation of different degrees according to the nature of the fault. It is for you not to deserve it. To accustom the fresh pupils to this idea, the last arrived has the charge of applying it at each week's great Tribunal. To begin with, it will be your duty. By your age and your knowledge you belong to the middle class, to the last year of this class. We unite the classes by an affectionate link, by which the pupils always benefit. I shall introduce you to Miss Angèle of the first class, who will be your great friend. Each senior pupil is thus attached to one of the middle class, and takes, in addition, into her care one of the junior class—a 'little mother' and 'little sister.' By and by you will get acquainted with the customs of the house."

Miss Juliette opened the door and I saw Miss Angèle, a fair, golden-haired girl of seventeen, very pretty, very coquettish, and very smiling; she embraced me tenderly and said: "Come, my dear, and get acquainted with your future friends and the mistress of your class."

I bowed to Miss Géraud and accompanied my new friend.

There was no end to my astonishment. My mistress, Miss Blanche Delorme, a charming red-haired girl of twenty, received me in the most amiable manner, and pulling my ear, said: "My darling, I only wish to be content with your work, and you will not have to complain of me. I have been Angèle's great friend when she belonged to the middle class, and I have been so happy about my education in this house, that I would not like to leave it again. Thus it is a school fellow you embrace when you kiss your mistress."

How far from the reception I had expected!

I then learned that the Misses Géraud's boarding school

was divided into three classes, each of thirteen pupils; the upper class included the boarders of fifteen to eighteen, the middle class those of twelve to fifteen, and the junior class the little ones of ten to twelve.

Pupils under ten were not received and the most affectionate care was taken of all degrees, and, according to physical development, of all ages.

Angèle introduced me to all her friends, who received me most kindly; I then became acquainted with the pupils of my own class, who showed themselves friendly and obliging; and at last I saw the little ones, who threw their arms about my neck. Among the latter I took note of the little Elisabeth, to whom Angèle was the "little mother" and to whom I should be the "little sister."

Besides Miss Blanche Delorme, I was introduced to Miss Nannette Courtelin, a brunette of twenty-two, with fiery eyes and a devilish manner, who is the mistress of the junior class, and to Miss Lucienne d'Herbollieu, mistress of the first class, who is a sentimental blonde of twenty-four, an ideal creature to devour with caresses.

My heart revelled in joy and pleasure. I foresaw happiness for every day of my new existence and resolved to do my best to merit it.

You now know almost all the persons, my dear Paul, and in my next letter you shall have an account of my friendly alliances and adventures. One dreams of a great many things in this house!

Yours,

Adelina

II
From the same to the same

Here I am, my dear Paul, introduced into real boarding school life, and at present I know a great many things of which I was before ignorant. I shall not conceal them from you, my own darling brother, so you may judge of my sincere affection.

The classical education of our establishment is much like that of other institutions; but it differs by its customs and usages and by a remarkable indulgence accorded to the senior girls, provided that they do not transgress the discipline of the school.

The second night after my arrival at the pension, half an hour before dinner time, I was about to finish my exercise, when I saw my friend Angèle enter and whisper some words to my mistress, Miss Blanche, who was reading.

She called me. "Have you finished your exercise, Adelina?" asked she.

"Yes, Madame."

"Well, we shall correct it tomorrow. Now Angèle wants you to keep her company, and I give you authority to follow her."

I perceived that the eyes of my little companions were beaming with mischief as I went away with her.

"I shall show you my little room," said she.

"You have a room of your own?"

"Yes, the seven eldest of the senior boarders sleep in their own rooms."

"That must be nice!"

"You will perhaps not always be of that opinion, dear!"

Angèle's room was small, but pretty and well furnished; it pleased me very much.

She invited me to sit down on her bed beside her, and

looked at me with such a tender expression in her eyes that I sighed and threw my arms about her neck.

She emitted a sweet perfume, which charmed me, and without having a clear understanding of what I did, I pressed my lips to hers.

"Tell me," whispered she, "did you allow yourself to be surprised while amusing yourself at home?"

"Yes," replied I, "and you?"

"I, too, was found out, but it is long ago; I was eleven years old, much younger than you, and I entered the lower class when I arrived here."

"With whom did you amuse yourself?"

"With my cousin, Hélène."

"But can girls amuse themselves with one another?"

"Oh yes, and pretty well, too, I assure you."

She kept me clasped to her bosom and I felt my heart throbbing; then she slipped her hand under my petticoats to the opening of my drawers.

I did not resist; a crowd of desires dinned in my ears.

She raised my shift and frigged me in a delicious manner while our lips were glued to one another.

During all these delightful diversions I forgot to reflect on the danger of being surprised a second time.

"You are hot-natured," said she. "You'll get many friends in the school."

"Come," I said in my turn, "let me look at you."

She smiled, withdrew her hand from my thighs, tucked up her skirts and thus exposed a little tuft of hair to my admiring eyes, besides a coquettish, wanton slit crying for a kiss; she showed me the fairness of her belly and putting her finger on her navel, said: "Kiss me there!"

I obeyed, my head all on fire. I applied a big kiss on the pretty mark; the sight of her thighs fascinated me; I bent over her, inhaling the effluvia of her body; she caressed my hair with her fingers while my face was glued to her silken skin; my cheeks became red with the heat and the intoxicating emotion. I felt she drew backwards as my tongue happened to touch her slit.

She started and said: "Go on a little quicker, that we may have time to spend."

I understood and licked, licked with a frantic passion, believing myself transferred to heaven.

She wriggled her arse, which I fondled with my hands, and all of a sudden she moistened my whole face; she spent, twisting herself as in cramp, and I did the same.

She rose quickly, ran to her dressing table, and we were just washing ourselves, when the bell rang for dinner.

"My darling," said she, "you have received the baptism of Love, you are now my little friend. Do not wonder at any thing, submit with docility to the punishments, speak to nobody of the scenes you will witness, and you will consider this establishment a real Olympus on earth."

We went downstairs and took each our seat at table.

The four mistresses dined with their pupils. Miss Blanche, who was already at her place, smiled and asked me. "Have you repeated your lesson before your great friend?"

"She has given me one which I shall never forget."

My answer pleased her; looking at me with very bright eyes she said: "You are a clever girl, try to prove so in everything."

I sat down, and my neighbour to the right, Marie Rougemont, a curly-haired brunette of fourteen, who has her bed beside mine in the dormitory, helped me to some soup, saying: "Did you know what Angèle confided to you?"

Guessing that the same friendly bond united all the pupils of the middle class to those of the first one, I answered: "Who is your great friend?"

"Isabelle Parmentier, the best pianist in the whole school, the little auburn thing, sitting next to Miss Lucienne."

"What a dear little wench!"

"Yes, but a wench with strong nerves; she is sixteen years old and is not afraid of remonstrating against all the seniors; she is a perfect little devil!"

Conversation is, as you will see, permitted at table, on condition that we are discreet, and do not disturb the serving nor inconvenience our fellow boarders.

Miss Juliette Géraud and her sister Fanny—the latter is twenty-seven years old—arrive generally in the midst of the meal; they superintend the tables, read the notes which they receive from the mistresses, speak to some of us and then retire, wishing us good night.

After dinner, which is served at half past seven, we have a semi-recreation in the drawing room till half past eight; the senior boarders read or are occupied with some fancy work, which they continue after our bedtime, for they sit up later than we do, a mistress or a senior girl tells fairy tales to the little ones, and those of the middle class talk in a low voice to some friends, or listen.

We are very fond of this hour because it gives an idea of what society is like. Our mistresses contrive to awaken our interest and give us now and then a piece of advice on good manners.

"No loud voices, my children," they repeat incessantly. "That's good for nothing but to spoil your throat and make you ridiculous and tired. Say gently, and in a low voice, what you have to say, be obliging to one another, thus you will facilitate a thousand chances of pleasure and enjoyment. Do not quarrel, and beware above all of such bad feelings as mistrust, jealousy, and envy."

The clock always strikes half past eight too soon, but as

sleep is close at our heels, we go to bed without too much regret.

We, the boarders of the middle class, sleep in two rows of seven beds each. The *chambre* is hung round with long curtains.

Miss Blanche has her room beside our dormitory and she leaves her door open all night.

Two lanterns of India paper light the room.

We have to undress in silence while our mistress is walking to and fro, inspecting the different particulars of our toilet. We undress behind the curtains, which are raised towards the foot of the bed and form a real little room or *chambrette*.

The mistress gives us the signal to turn into bed by clapping her hands; then she recites a Benedicite, continues her walk for a few minutes longer, and at last retires to her own room.

That night she had scarcely left us when my curtain moved and I caught sight of the head of Marie Rougemont, who, with a finger on her lips, signed to me not to speak or make a noise.

I did not move and awaited the adventure, which I knew must be coming.

Marie advanced cautiously, entered into the free space between the curtain and my bed, and, stooping down, inspected the dormitory to see if she risked being surprised.

Miss Blanche's room was opposite to my bedstead.

She looked towards this room and having heard the rustling noise of the mistress turning in bed, she approached, kissed my lips, and said: "Turn and show me your bottom. I should like to lick it. I have a great liking in that way and you must have a pretty one, since men used to amuse themselves with it."

33

Our legend increased, it was no longer one man, a little bit of a man, my brother, you, Paul, that they attributed to me, but *men*.

I never thought of rectifying her mistake, my mind was all occupied on the luscious pleasure; I turned according to her wish, raised my sheets and night-gown and presented her my already boiling buttocks.

Oh, what skill, my dear! No, you cannot imagine how artfully she proceeded! She did not tell a lie, when she said she loved bums.

She began by framing it with her arms, applying sometimes one, sometimes the other cheek on each buttock; she then pinched her nose by gradually opening and stretching the furrow with her fingers; she tried to penetrate as deep as possible, just as you did the first time you know, then she stopped, rose on tip-toe, and caressed it with the points of her very firm bubbies; at last she kissed it tenderly and then licked the whole furrow, sighing and trembling more and more violently. In her felicity she forgot to be prudent.

The bed creaked under our voluptuous movements, and all on a sudden the shell burst, the curtains opened and Miss Blanche appeared.

Without saying a word, she put her hand on Marie's shoulder and then whispered in a low voice: "This is very naughty, Marie; you might awaken your companions and cause them to commit the same folly. You are culpable doubly because you have addressed yourself to a fresh pupil who does not know the rules. Dress and follow me to the room of correction! Tomorrow you will have to appear before Miss Fanny. You, Adelina, ought to have repelled your neighbour's propositions. You have not done so and deserve a correction. For this once you will sustain the simple flogging without appearing before the Tribunal.

Tomorrow you will have to accompany me to the head-mistress.

I was terrified.

Marie dressed without making a single protestation and went away with Miss Blanche.

I turned from one side to another for a long while; Morpheus took it into his head to avoid me. Exhaustion however at last got the better of my insomnia.

My letter is already very long, my dear little Paul; next time I shall tell you of my further experiences.

Yours,

Adelina

III
From the same to the same

When I awoke next morning at six o'clock, I was in a mortal fright.

As soon as prayers were over, and the pupils had returned to the school rooms, Miss Blanche conducted me to a large place, entirely hung with black draperies and lighted by a six-armed chandelier.

Miss Fanny was sitting before a small table. She wore a black silk dress which was exceedingly becoming and set off her fair beauty—she was as pretty as her sister—without taking away any of the austerity of her aspect.

Miss Nannette Courtelin stood before the table in the middle of the room; on a sofa I perceived Marie Rouge-mont. I was invited to sit down beside her on another sofa.

The hall was only furnished with sofas and *prie-dieus* of different size and form.

Blanche approached Miss Fanny, with whom she exchanged a few words, and then took her place beside Miss Nannette. Our great principal delivered the following address: "Your fault, Marie, is greater than Adelina's. It comes within the jurisdiction of the Tribunal and you will have to render account for it tomorrow. But being culpable at the same time as Adelina, you will have to assist at her punishment, in order that you may both keep it in mind. You, Adelina, are not ignorant of the kind of fault you have committed by not opposing resistance to your neighbour's solicitations. It is the more grave because you risked disturbing the sleep of your companions. As we have nothing else to reproach you with, either with regard to your application at school or as to your conduct, you shall come off for this once with some good slaps on your posteriors, inflicted here before the restricted committee. If you commit the same fault a second time you will be flogged with the rod in presence of the three united classes and the High Administerial Council. I need not dwell upon how painful this punishment would be to your self-respect. Thank your mistress for the moderation she has shown in regard to your fault, and promise not to begin again."

I was greatly moved, promised what she asked, and did not refuse to kiss Miss Blanche.

Miss Nannette was charged with the execution of the chastisement.

A *prie-dieu* was advanced, I knelt on the rather high stool, my arms and legs were tied, Miss Fanny turned my petticoats over my back, and as they had made me take off my drawers, my stark-naked bum appeared in all its plumpness.

All these preparations were very impressive. I blushed to the roots of my hair and a sense of shame paralysed my brain. I dared not look at anybody. All on a sudden a terrible cuff fell on my buttocks.

I set up a cry. Miss Nannette had a hard hand. My arse trembled under the vibrating agitation of her hand, but she did not stop at that.

She gave me three, four, five, ten, twelve slaps, striking as hard as she could. I was half mad with excitement. I screamed; I implored their pardon; everything whirled round about me; it seemed as if my flesh was torn asunder and I had no doubt but that my poor arse would be injured for ever.

The chastisement was over. Miss Fanny was standing before me, to the left I perceived Miss Nannette and to the right Miss Blanche.

At a sign of Miss Fanny, Marie Rougemont rose and threw herself down behind me. Then our form-mistress said: "The punishment of this dear treasure is attributable to you, Marie; kiss it, please, and soothe the pain it suffers."

Was it possible?

After the chastisement the reason that had occasioned it was authorised. My tears were dried as if by magic. Marie caressed me gently. By and by I recovered my senses and distinguished near to us Miss Blanche squatting upon the ground between the thighs of Miss Fanny, whose clothes were tucked up. She was kissing her as you did me.

Then Miss Nannette gathered up her skirts on her arm, approached the two women and showed them her legs and her stark-naked arse, and Miss Fanny caressed it with her hand, while Miss Blanche from time to time turned and licked the bottom.

Marie Rougemont's endearments made me go into ecstasies; forgetting the sufferings through which I had passed, I was not long in spending.

On discharging, Marie gave me a more hearty kiss than before and then interrupted her caresses. She approached the three women who, arrayed in a row, offered her their posteriors, which she licked one after the other.

Attached to the *prie-dieu* I thought that I was enjoying a charming dream.

I admired three female fundaments capable of inspiring the most violent desires; my sighs became more and more frequent; I got agitated and cursed the hands that tied me.

Miss Blanche understood my feelings; she called in mind my situation and kindly came to release me.

She pointed at Marie, who sat upon her heels behind the buttocks of Miss Fanny and Miss Nannette, caressing them in equal proportions; she tucked up her clothes and presented me her own.

Oh, my dear little Paul, I understood at that moment the pleasure you and the Abbé felt, when you devoured my arse with your burning kisses.

Blanche's bum, plump, round, with a well-marked furrow between the buttocks and a downy beard below, was exposed to my enchanted eyes in all its dazzling whiteness.

She bent forward to allow me to admire all its sweet contours and I kissed with emotion the fleshy parts, while I directed my hand between her thighs to her pretty little cunt which appeared between the hair.

She rounded her arse more and more, the furrow reflected a thousand glowing fires, one of my fingers found its way into it, then my nose and at length my lips and my tongue.

What a glow, what bliss! I was beside myself with joy when all of a sudden it was taken from me. I had however not even the time to complain before the arse of Nannette drew up before my enraptured eyes.

Oh, what a gait it had! It was not so big as that of Blanche; but one would think that it had a soul, so much did it humour the passions. It was elegant, of a perfect, oval shape, firm and hard, full of nerves and muscles and she changed the furrow between the buttocks with wonderful dexterity. The latter welled out suddenly and then contracted, the furrow opened very much and then shut violently, showing but a fine line, into which it seemed impossible to slip even the tip of a nail.

Wriggled with an incredible skill, the arse heaved up and sank down, turning to the right and to the left, and in love with all these charms my tongue followed it in all its evolutions, moistening it with the saliva mounting in my throat.

What a heavenly game, what a charming solution of the pain!

I was favoured with Fanny's, too, at the same time as that of Marie Rougemont. The latter lay down on all fours and our great principal placed herself upon her, but a little more forward.

I had to divide my caresses between these two new jewels.

Fanny's arse was much fuller and of a more perfect shape than that of Marie and yet Marie's was not without grace and beauty. Protected by our principal's splendid bum, the biggest of those viewed in the hall, it seemed to affect modesty and timidity and it claimed as well as the big one the contact of my eager lips.

But how is it possible to describe Fanny's royal beauty? Oh, my darling Paul, you would have wallowed upon it in frantic bliss. I asked myself, how she who has such well-shaped limbs and such a delicate form could have such a big arse!

Exposed in this manner it dominated her whole body; its furrow was deep, well-marked and rosy, it continued very far down and upwards and was big enough to engulf the whole affair of the Abbé.

When she was standing it assumed natural and reasonable limits; when on all fours it increased in size so that I grew mad about it.

Returning from time to time to my little friend below, I clung to it with my hands, mouth, tongue, and teeth; she leaped with it, discharging already, and murmured: "My little Adelina, you will become one of our best pupils, we shall all be fond of you and you will get to like our school. Give me the slaps, dear, which Nannette gave you."

I dared not. I kissed and I licked. Nannette pushed my head against Fanny's arse, saying: "Why, thrash on, little one, she wants you to do so, and you will procure her great sensual rapture by it."

While I set to work, striking one blow after another on her pretty arse, which responded to each cuff by a shivering down the furrow, Nannette took Blanche astride on her knees, one glueing her lips to the other's. Their hands got under their petticoats and they frigged one another furiously, rubbing their bellies together.

At a certain moment Fanny squeezed Marie's arse between her thighs, heaved up, and then fell down, suddenly crushing the latter under the weight of her body while she discharged her liquor of Lust.

I was rivetted to the spot with bliss and my tongue remained between her buttocks.

Is it not wonderful, my dear, that I have come so well off? Keep the secret of our correspondence well, and you shall always be kept *au courant* of every thing that happens.

Your loving sister,

Adelina

IV
From the same to the same

The last thing of which I told you, my Paul, was the rapture that took possession of my whole body, when I lay in ecstasy behind Fanny's bum.

By and by we composed ourselves; a curtain was drawn aside, a charming dressing room appeared and we entered to clean ourselves.

Miss Fanny embraced us all and retired. Just as I thought that the *séance* must be over, Miss Blanche asked me to accompany her to her room; Nannette led away Marie.

When we arrived at her room Blanche gave me the permission to call her by her Christian name except when in school. She made me strip stark naked and she did the same. We turned into bed and she took me in her arms, clasping my buttocks with both her hands; I took hold of hers in the same way. She offered me her lips, which I hastened to kiss and suck; her most charming bubbies were pressed to my bosom, her belly was glued to mine; it was an endless ecstasy, in which we lay without stirring, pressed against one another as if to mix our flesh together, inhaling one another's breathing in an uninterrupted series of kisses, suckings, and tonguings.

In Heaven the bliss and felicity cannot be greater!

Our hands only left our buttocks to wander over each other's bodies, or to permit our arms to hug one another closer.

To obtain such an end of the punishment I was ready to commit the same fault every night.

Blanche guessed as much, and said: "My dear Adelina, in spite of all our present happiness you must not sin again. To be worthy of the luscious delight I give you—and which you will obtain in this school according to the progress you

41

make—it is necessary to take care of your health and not to compromise your companions! By exposing yourself to an illness, you expose your companions and your mistresses to a misfortune which you afterwards will regret your whole life. We might have treated you severely and have deprived you of this luxury, which opens Heaven to you; we have not done so, in order to prove that your sensual desires will be gratified, when the hour is come, but on condition that you do not violate the wise rules which maintain peace and friendship between the pupils and secure us their submission and their effort to please us. If we did not prohibit the nightly encounters, not one of the boarders would sleep. Now you know our indulgence with regard to pleasures. Don't abuse it. Can I reckon on your obedience?"

"Oh yes, my dear mistress."

"We know that you have excellent health, and we shall help you to recover your strength by a hygiene prescribed by one of our physicians. Convinced of your zeal and your good intentions we shall not grudge you the occasions of pleasure. Beware of adventures with capricious schoolfellows. I confide it to you here: a mere trifle will inform us of the fault and it will be stopped at its commencement. Next time we shall be merciless."

We never ceased kissing one another while we frigged our cunts and Blanche soon fell into a passion. Jumping out of bed, she opened a drawer.

"Look," said she, "put this around your waist and I'll teach you how to be my little lover."

"Oh," said I, "I know how that is done. It is put into the bumhole."

"You have had it in there!" she said, and burst out laughing.

"Yes," replied I.

"Poor little thing, how you must have suffered."

"No, it was very nice."

"Really! We will try that another day. At present it is not the bumhole you'll have to put it in, but here between my thighs."

"Will it enter there?"

"Come quick upon me, my darling! Move at the same time. This toy is called a dildo and it serves as a substitute for a man; you have poured such a fire into my veins that I must have a good fuck this instant."

Such lessons are not difficult to learn!

Blanche had put the tip of the instrument in her cunt. She wriggled in the maddest manner and I imitated her as best I could. The rather big instrument soon disappeared in her belly.

We were locked in each other's arms; we shivered in turns; she devoured me with her kisses, which I returned with passion; a penetrating fire burnt my spinal cord and we discharged at the same time; our spendings mixed together in our hair.

"You promise to be very good," said she, when we were dressing.

"I swear it."

"I trust your word and you shall not repent of it."

Afterwards we returned to our class.

Two of the elder boarders, Berthe Litton and Josèphine de Branzier, had replaced the mistresses absent.

Marie Rougemont was already at her place. Neither she nor the other pupils spoke of anything to me. Everything went on as if nothing had happened.

During the recreation I was astonished not to see my great friend, Angèle. I was sorry to hear that my fault in

part recoiled upon her, and that she would be punished the
next day on my account. She was shut up alone and had to
work all the day.

This was the way they exerted influence on our morals
and our hearts in order to stop our errors!

The following day would be that of the Tribunal, and I
should be introduced into the particulars of the life at
school.

The Tribunal sat at five o'clock p.m.

My mistress, Miss Blanche, took me to a small parlour,
where I was introduced to the Chaplain, the Rev. Mr.
Jacquart; to Messrs. Camille Grandin, Jules Callas, and
Bérnard de Charvey, physician to the school. They were all
men between thirty-five and forty years old, belonging to
the High Administerial Council of the house.

I was very bashful and bowed awkwardly, but they were
all so kind that I soon took courage again.

Misses Juliette and Fanny Géraud, the two other form-
mistresses, and a pupil from the Superior Class, Berthe
Litton, soon after joined us.

We went into the room of correction, arranged in quite
another way than the day before.

At the upper end of the hall five armchairs served as a
box. The Chaplain was sitting in the middle. He had on his
right hand Miss Juliette and on his left hand Miss Fanny.
Mr. Camille Grandin was sitting beside the former, Dr.
Bérnard de Charvey beside the latter.

The three form-mistresses sat down on chairs to the left,
Berthe Litton, Mr. Jules Callas and I, to the right.

Opposite to the five armchairs at the other end of the
room were rows of chairs for the pupils, who however, were
not present at the beginning of the chastisement.

Those who had deserved the flagellation without their
friend being present were first punished. The lower class

opened the *séance* with a pretty brunette, Lisa Carrin, who was brought in stark naked, by one of the two superintendents, Miss Elise Robert, a tall splendid girl of nineteen. The other, Miss Georgette Pascal, a pretty little blonde of eighteen, was a great contrast to the former, who was a vigorous brunette with a light, not at all unbecoming, down on her upper lip.

The little Lisa was all scarlet, very unhappy and perplexed; she approached snivelling, and was fastened to a seat in the middle of the hall, her back turned to the Council.

Berthe rose, took a slip of paper from the table and read: "Miss Lisa Carrin has given one of her companions a box on the ear, has answered again when her mistress scolded her, has refused to copy the ten pages given to her as a punishment. She has suffered the privation of recreation and has been condemned to receive five slaps on her buttocks before the Council. Miss Adelina Mirzan is charged with the execution."

Dear me! After having suffered flagellation myself, I had to apply it on her and that in the presence of all these people.

A terrible fright rivetted me to the spot; my legs trembled. A profound silence pervaded the assembly. The white skin of the little culprit dazzled my eyes. Miss Juliette addressed me as follows: "Well, Adelina, make a decision. Don't prolong the anxiety of the child by your cruel and useless hesitation. Strike her, and strike hard; she has well deserved it."

All eyes rested upon me; I could not put it off any longer.

I rose and approached the terrible stake.

Poor little Lisa! Her frail legs supported a pretty little white fundament. She trembled with fear and said in a low voice: "Don't strike too hard, pray; I am so afraid of the blows."

It cut me to the heart. Miss Juliette continued: "Go on, go on, Adelina! You set to work with deplorable slowness, we shall never finish if you don't make haste. This is nothing compared with the others."

I thought for a minute of refusing to strike, but I had a faint idea that not only I, but all those who were to be punished that day, would smart for it.

I closed my eyes, and one, two, five smacks resounded on her little arse. Lisa set up a cry; I had not spared her as I intended to do. Her bottom was all crimson.

She was released and brought away.

"Remain where you are," commanded Miss Juliette. "There are two other culprits, who must be punished in the same way."

Alas, the next was no other than Angèle, who appeared in all her clothes, looking very sad.

Her arms and legs were tied and the upper part of her body was supported by the back of a *prie-dieu*.

Berthe read: "Miss Angèle de Noirmont is condemned to twelve slaps on her buttocks for the nightly lubricity of her young friend Adelina who was surprised in *flagrant délit* with Marie Rougemont. One day's privation of all pleasures for not having taught Adelina the nature of the moral ties which bind them together."

Her petticoats were tucked up and pinned to her shoulders; her pretty arse appeared—divine, enchanting, bewitching!

Oh, how much I should have preferred to kiss it! But I had to obey. Miss Juliette said: "Strike, Adelina, and proceed a little quicker than you did before."

I gave her two or three slaps with evident irresolution.

The Chaplain protested. "It is no longer a chastisement

when you strike so leniently. Don't spare your friend or you'll expose her to being flogged with the rod."

Angèle did not say a word. I set to work and struck harder and harder.

It seemed to me that she shivered, her buttocks trembled and she agitated her thighs. To my great astonishment she discharged suddenly at my eleventh slap.

How? This commotion turned to a felicity to her! I could scarcely believe my own eyes and by an effect of sympathy I thrilled with pleasure. I struck the twelfth cuff with surprising violence.

Angèle was released; she kissed me and went away.

The third culprit was another of the senior pupils, Miss Ève Philippe, condemned to flagellation with the rod for a discussion with her form-mistress, Miss Lucienne d'Herbollieu.

She was placed like Angèle and they handed me a scourge with five or six lashes.

Ève was beautifully made and her skin was of dazzling whiteness. With her extremely coquettish and slender form, her blue eyes of angelic purity, she represented the *beau idéal* of all blondes. Her arse was a fine shape, less full than those of the mistresses of which I had had a glimpse the day before, but nevertheless quite perfect, and again I could not make up my mind to tarnish such a charming body.

I heard the command, my arm rose and sank, the lashes fell blow upon blow, scourging her two buttocks, penetrating to the midst of her thighs, and exciting long cries from the malefactor, who, wriggling from one side to the other, sued for pardon.

"No, no mercy," cried Miss Juliette, "strike harder. At Ève's age it is not permitted to commit the fault of quarrelling with one's mistress who only strives to be kind to her pupils. The nearer the day for leaving school approaches, the more she ought to show herself grateful and deferential for the kindness she has met with there."

"I promise never to do it again, ma'am. I ask your pardon, oh, Lucienne!"

"Strike, Adelina, till the blood flows."

I struck with all my might; my eyes grew misty. The flesh of this charming arse moved up and down; it thrilled me through; my face became flushed and in spite of myself my free hand contracted on my dress between my thighs; in proportion as I struck I frigged myself.

Nobody seemed to notice it. My temper got the better of me. Ève cried, sobbed and murmured: "You wicked, wicked girl! Who would have thought you were so hard-hearted. Oh, enough, no more, I beseech you to stop."

Her blood was flowing; the punishment was done, my scarlet face grew pale. Ève's wounded arse was cleaned and dressed, she was released, and had to kiss me as a proof that she would forget the pain.

She went out and I was called before the Council.

Then, my dear Paul, Juliette tucked up my clothes and attested my emotion. I was handed from one to another of all these gentlemen, who caressed my thighs and my buttocks, patted my cheeks, and promised me a thousand pleasures, if I would be very docile and very discreet.

You cannot imagine how happy I was! They might have asked me whatever they liked, I should have refused nothing.

But the *séance* was not yet over, every one returned to his place and all the classes entered.

But this is enough for today, my dear, tomorrow the other details.

Your loving sister,

Adelina

V
From the same to the same

Opposite to the Council, my dear Paul, the three classes took their seats; the little ones on the first row of chairs, then the middle class, and at last the elder boarders.

I observed that some of the pupils wore a red dress with a cross of honour on their breast.

Later on I learned that they belonged to the confraternity of Red Girls; they enter into a league with the school, swearing never to marry but with a husband presented by our mistresses and always to assist at the great feasts of the confraternity.

Two of the little ones wore this dress, three of the middle class, and six of the superior class.

Everybody desired it; it was only given to the most meritorious, the most intelligent and the most discreet after a certain time of trial and according to certain rules, about which a thousand curious things are whispered.

In this assembly of pupils brought up upon such kind principles, the most profound silence reigned.

Two young girls of the middle class appeared before the High Council: Marie Rougemont and another by the name of Désirée Brocart. The latter had been surprised in the water closet enjoying solitary pleasures.

Marie appeared dressed in a long white nightgown, hanging down to her feet, and with dishevelled hair; her hands were tied behind her back.

She was placed standing before the Council, and the Chaplain said: "We know of the disgraceful act you have committed, and shall not mention it here; your fault cannot be overlooked. Before we define the punishment, we desire to hear what you have to say in your defence."

"The blood mounted into my head; my nerves were so

much excited, I was not in possession of my usual mental activity. I suffered from sleeplessness; different thoughts troubled me the whole day; I feared that I should fall ill, if I had not done that with which you reproach me. I am sorry for it and I accept the penance you will inflict upon me. I shall not grumble, but I am afraid I cannot prevent myself from doing it again, and I prefer to confess immediately, at the same time beseeching you to be indulgent in the future."

"For this time we condemn you to flagellation with the rod, and to be whipped with a switch three days running before you go to bed. You will be separated one month from your schoolfellows and a fortnight from your great friend."

"Oh, I beseech you, do not isolate me for such a long time!"

"Besides, we condemn your friend Isabelle Parmentier to flagellation with the cat-o'-nine-tails, which she shall suffer at your side. The judgment is final."

At these words Isabelle Parmentier was introduced in the same attire as Marie.

They were placed opposite to one another, tied to a *prie-dieu*, their nightgowns were gathered up and pinned to their shoulders. It fell to my lot to flog Isabelle, while Miss Nannette punished Marie.

A fresh bottom offered itself to my contemplation, a nervous one with round, projecting buttocks, and a furrow well marked at the top and below, where a thicket of very black hair appeared.

Isabelle, who by her slender size conveyed the impression of being but a child, presented when thus seen limbs of no common vigour. Her well-developed calves attracted notice to her beautiful legs and the blameless magnificent slope of her loins, while her exquisite shoulders and the projection of her nightgown betrayed firm and bold breasts.

As I became more experienced, I began to enjoy the flogging.

However pretty it might be, Isabelle's arse received, as well as Ève's, plenty of cuts with the scourge. She did not cry, but started now and then, in contrast to Marie, who screamed loudly at each lash of the switch.

Immediately after this execution, Désirée Brocart entered, dressed like her two predecessors; she carried a chamber pot in her hand.

The sight was so droll that the whole assembly burst out laughing, which produced a scarlet blush on her cheeks.

They made her sit down on a sofa and the chamber pot was placed on a stool beside her.

Miss Nannette put a looking-glass into the vessel. Then the Chaplain said: "My dear child, filthiness is a very nice thing, but there are places more convenient for appreciating the charms and the sweetness of it than that in which you took refuge. As your fault is positively personal, it does not entail other consequences upon your great friend than that of being obliged to flog you herself. Your punishment will be more moral than effective. This charming recipient shall be put on your head, and you will receive twelve slaps from Diane de Verson's pretty hands. For eight days you will have to take your meals at the end of the table and this little furniture will be placed beside the dishes to remind you of the place where you amused yourself. After your flagellation you shall take a walk through the three classes, your pot in your hand, and you must bring it back, whether it is full or no, to clean it along with the little looking-glass, which you will find at the bottom, and which shall adorn the head of your bed for a whole month."

The hilarity became general even among the members of the Council, and Désirée blushed more and more, quite beside herself with shame and bashfulness.

The pot was put on her head and her friend Diane slapped her violently, crying: "That's for you, naughty, stupid girl; shame on you! Is it permitted to shut oneself up in such a shameful place when one can have such nice company? Dirty little wench! Next time I'll ask our mistress to break our friendship."

"Oh, no, no, Diane, I'll never do so again; slap harder, if you like, but do forgive me!"

Her walk with the pot completed the mirth. Almost all the little ones pretended to be in need of it, and almost all of them sent some trickling drops into the vase. The middle class and the elder pupils showed more decency. Nevertheless the pot was filled.

It was brought to the Chaplain, who taking it in his hand, looked at the culprit and said: "What would you think if I ordered you to drink it?"

Désirée cried silently.

He continued: "If I did so, it would seem as if I approved the villainous act of which you are guilty. I might also command it to be poured over your body and condemn you to stay in the dirt a whole night. You merit such a filthy punishment; but I dispense with it. Go, clean the pot and don't sin again."

The punishments done, they proceeded to the recompenses.

After the reading of the good marks, the names of those who had distinguished themselves were repeated. They began with the senior pupils.

1. The Pink Ribbon was assigned to Miss Athénaïs Caffarel for continued application and exemplary conduct in the school room and her unceasing desire to help the

Direction and the form-mistresses in the care and service of the school.

She was a blonde of seventeen years six months, in possession of her first diploma and belonging to the school since her tenth year.

2. Admitted into the confraternity of Red Girls was Miss Angèle de Noirmont (my great friend) for her bland character, her attachment to her mistresses and the school, the perfection of her studies, and her precious assistance in removing difficulties among the pupils.

3. Miss Eulalie Pierre, thirteen years and six months old, and

4. Miss Lénore Grécoeur, fourteen years old, have the permission to go to bed at ten o'clock and to get up at seven for a whole week.

5. Miss Anne Flavart shall receive a book of fairy tales for her application and obedience.

6. Miss Pauline de Merbes, ten and a half years old (a very lively and passionate girl), shall be admitted into the confraternity of Red Girls, for the readiness and invincible energy with which she tries to make progress and follow the counsels of her mistresses.

Afterwards the Chaplain made a little speech of congratulation and Miss Juliette said some words also, after which all of us, except the mistresses and the Red Girls, left the hall of correction.

While waiting for dinner we played in a glass-covered court-yard under the surveillance of Miss Élise Robert.

Though the three classes were united, we keenly felt the absence of those who had remained with the High Administerial Council and the mistresses.

Miss Robert amused herself with the little ones, those of the middle class chattered with their great friends, I joined a group of five or six of my classmates and tried to gather further information as to the customs of the boarding school.

I no longer belonged to the ignorant; I had but to go before the wind.

Now, my dear little Paul, you know everything about my entrance at the Misses Géraud's. Await patiently another series of letters, which will inform you of my next experiences. I shall not conceal any of my adventures from you. It is delightful to tell you about them.

If you are deprived of carnal pleasures in London I wish you to enjoy them, at least in imagination, with me. My letters are imbued with the fire of my senses; I shall always consider it a privilege to gratify your sensual desires. Do not fall ill, my darling; sooner or later we shall recommence the pleasures they meant to defraud us of. I promise you that with all my heart.

A thousand kisses from your loving sister,

Yours,

Adelina

Chapter Three
The Nocturnal Feast

I
From Adelina to Paul

How fast time runs, when all one's dreams and one's desires are fulfilled. It is more than three months, my dear Paul, since I wrote my last letter and what has not happened since then!

I know you have received my letters by our cousin Eulalie, your schoolfellow at the Jesuits', who was called to Paris by the death of a relative. Destroy them as soon as you have read them, otherwise they might get us into trouble and we might be obliged to cease our dear confidential correspondence.

I hope you enjoy yourself as much as I do; in any case I send you the account of my intoxicatingly luscious combats to show you that my sentiments about those nice things have not changed. I am very often sorry for you, which is a proof that my heart is not yet corrupted by selfishness.

Our regular and well-organized life is not fatiguing and we have all sorts of pleasures and pleasant surprises.

Besides the ties of friendship attaching us to our great friend, we have several charming little intrigues.

One morning a few weeks after my arrival I found a letter in my desk, which set my heart throbbing violently. Isabelle Parmentier, Marie Rougemont's great friend, wrote as follows:

My dear Adelina,

You have scourged my arse in the prettiest manner possible and you have almost spoiled my pretty bum I dare say; nevertheless, I bear you no ill will, oh no, far from that! Marie has told me that you are very lustful and so am I. My desire of your person is great and I should be very happy if your lips would obliterate the memory of the cuts you gave my buttocks. If you long for my charms as I do for yours, it is easy to meet without running the risk of being punished. Ask to go to confession tomorrow. I have to arrange the altar for Sunday. If you arrive at the chapel at four o'clock we shall have half an hour to ourselves. The Chaplain never arrives till half past four. If you consent, my darling, I beg you to put a blue bow in your hair this evening before entering the refectory.

Your friend,
Isabelle

I put on the blue ribbon and the next day at four o'clock I went to the chapel. Isabelle was waiting for me. She took me by the hand and led me along to the sacristy. There she opened another door and we entered the most charming little boudoir.

She threw her arms around me and though she is smaller than I am, lifted me like a feather from the ground. Then, throwing me on a divan, she said: "Be quick, show me if you are as well made as Marie says."

Her hand wandered over my thighs and my buttocks, she opened my drawers, approached her lips and with a wonderful agility dived her tongue into all the pleasant places.

Rising, she tucked up her own clothes and exhibited her buttocks deprived of every trace of drawers, and, as I was lying on the divan, she applied her bottom to my face and ordered me to suck it.

"Suck everywhere," said she. "You cruel, naughty girl who struck so hard the other day. Look, it revenges itself, it pinches your nose, like that; yes, try to find the orifice. I love this tickling! Oh, you little minx, you are quite an adept. Yes, clasp it in your hands, more, more, do you feel it against your cheeks? Marie's passionate love of bums made me delight in such caresses. Oh, you make progress! What do you want, when you twist me like that? Which is the prettiest, my arse or Angèle's?"

"I have scarcely looked at Angèle's!"

"What a joke! What do you do, when you retire together?"

"She is fond of caressing me and when it is my turn, she prefers the front."

"How funny! She always wanted your predecessor to suck her nipples. Angèle is indeed fanciful! Yes, yes, but don't stop your caresses. If you have not seen the arse of

your great friend, you must have seen others, that of
Blanche, for instance; do you prefer it to mine?"

"It is bigger, but it cannot twist about like yours."

"Oh, you appreciate that, do you? It is always on fire,
and I should like a tongue between my buttocks all day
long."

"With such a disposition, Marie must get her fill."

"Marie prefers an arse that does not move, and mine is
never quiet when it is well handled. She always gets into
trouble because she affects nocturnal adventures. She likes
them because the fear of being surprised prevents those to
whom she applies from stirring. She throws herself flat
upon their arse and licks it softly with her tongue and lips."

"It is funny that one can never be at one with her."

"I should be at one with you, I must say! You are bold
and mutinous and you manage your tongue with real skill.
Will you be my little sweetheart?"

"And Angèle?"

"Angèle will remain your official friend. We all have our
secret sweethearts and Angèle like the others."

"Indeed! Angèle has a sweetheart?"

"You don't know all the stories of the house, I see!
Angèle's late great friend, Blanche, has taken a fancy to her.
They often sleep together, and it is owing to this
circumstance that you were seized with Marie."

"Oh!"

"Yes. If Marie had spoken to me that day, I should have
advised her to put off her visit till a night when Blanche had
gone to Angèle."

"They change rooms?"

"At least twice a week."

The licking and sucking continued; we only ceased in
time to be in the chapel the very moment the Chaplain
arrived.

I consented to be the sweetheart of the little devil, who promised me any quantity of voluptuous bliss.

It was the first time I had been to confession at the boarding school.

In that respect the pupils in their teens have free scope provided that they go to communion at fixed epochs.

I had only seen the Chaplain at the *séances* of punishment and at the Divine Offices.

I entered the little niche in a very quiet frame of mind, and after the Pater noster, and the Ave, the Chaplain said: "It is wise of you, my child, to remember the utility of my ministry. You want to confess some small faults, I suppose?"

"Your advice will be precious to me, my Father. I wanted to consult you long ago."

"Speak, my child, you may be convinced that I take the greatest interest in your trouble."

"My ideas are somewhat confused. I came to this school in consequence of an adventure, of which you cannot be ignorant, my Father, and here I find, that the thing for which they intended to punish me at home, is almost authorised. Where is the good and where is the evil? I don't know."

"Your heart will show it you, my child. Be obedient to your superiors, maintain the harmony between those around you, respect everybody's opinion; be silent as to what might hurt your fellow-creatures' feelings and try to give your friends every possible joy and felicity."

"I understand, my Father. The thing is to practise the morals of the place in which we live and never to contradict the ideas of those on whom we depend."

The Chaplain was puzzled for a minute or two; then he continued: "The evil consists in mistaking our reciprocal wants. This house is governed by rules which are very different from those observed by other boarding schools. You are a clever girl. You will not compromise your present happiness by fruitless debates. Amuse yourself, my child, and try to amuse the others according to the rules of the school. I remit your sins unto you."

"I thank you, my Father; and I testify my gratitude by acknowledging that the confession has served me as pretext for joining a friend who had given me a voluptuous rendez-vous.

He smiled and replied: "I do not wish to know the name of your accomplice. As a penitence for your trick you must, however, calm the irritation of the poor excited devil here between my thighs. Look, my child."

I leaned my forehead against the grate and saw the Chaplain with raised cassock, exhibiting a very, very, long and stiff instrument.

"How can I calm it, my Father?"

"By sucking it in the sacristy. Will you yield to the penitence?"

"If I had a right to refuse, I should ask as a favour to do so."

"Oh, my child, you promise to be a splendid recruit to the school. Then, come to the sacristy."

"Why to the sacristy, my Father? If I joined you in your little cell and knelt down before you?"

"Yes, yes, that's it."

Isabelle was still at the altar. She turned at the noise of the door of the confessional, and stood disconcerted when she saw me disappear beside the Chaplain.

I knelt down between his thighs; he caressed my head and hair. My lips approached that big thing. I longed for this pleasure. I had not had the male thing since I left Chartres. I blessed my own intelligence, which had ushered me into the presence of the Chaplain's attributes. The enormous head entered my mouth; my heart leaped with joy and happiness, and I took hold of the sprinkler with both hands.

What a size it was, my dear Paul! Twice as big as the Abbé Dussal's and three times as big as yours.

I applied my lips to it slowly, and glided down by sudden jerks till I little by little engulfed the splendid monster in my mouth.

Alas! I could not take it all in. Thrown back in his chair, his thighs completely uncovered, the Chaplain resigned himself to my caresses. I could not resist the intoxicating temptation to enjoy to the full the contact of his naked body. I let the thing slip out of my mouth, placed my forehead under it, raised the balls with my tongue, and stooped to lick as far as the beginning of his buttocks.

He sighed again and again.

He patted my head with his knob to remind me of the sucking, and I resumed my work with lips and tongue.

He started wriggling his arse, and from time to time squeezed down the upper part of my body by pressing his hands on my shoulders, and suddenly a mighty jet of sperm (the name of the male liquor, as he told me) was sent into my mouth and over my nose and cheeks.

Oh, the trembling and jumping of his prick on my face! I shall never forget it. It throbbed so violently that I thought it would break my teeth and bruise my face.

I lay with my head on his thighs in a delicious ecstasy; he caressed my cheeks, which I glued to his naked body, and then wiped my face with his handkerchief. I understood that we had to blot out the traces of the adventure.

Some drops had stained my bodice. He let down his cassock and told me to accompany him to the sacristy, where he would clean it.

We went out of the confessional and when we passed the

altar, I observed that Isabelle, who was hidden on the other side, sent me an angry look.

In the sacristy the Chaplain took out the stain on my bodice with some water. I washed my face in order that nothing might betray me and left him after he had kissed me tenderly and promised me his protection.

In a passage between the chapel and the court-yard I came across Isabelle, who seized me by the arm and boxed my ears and cried: "There, you dirty beast, sucker that you are. You are not content with your friends; you want to play with the men. That's to teach you better manners. It is all over between us, you know, and never fear! I'll speak to Angèle and she'll give it to you."

She turned her back upon me and left me quite stunned; I thought one ought to try one's hand at all pleasures and here one of them gave me an enemy.

Another vexation awaited me in the study. On my return Miss Blanche said, with a certain irony: "Your confession has been rather long, Adelina. You had really so many sins to confess? I should not have thought so. They have, however, been rather important, I see; you look quite distracted and your manners are strange. I deprive you of the recreations of tomorrow and I beg you to copy the whole of the first act of *Athalie*. The verses will speak of poetry to your soul."

This awakening was rather disagreeable, my dear Paul; but I submitted in silence.

A hearty kiss from your sister,

Adelina

II
From the same to the same

The Chaplain had promised me his protection; he kept his word.

It was some days before he got an opportunity of occupying himself with my humble person; but one morning, after he had heard of the punishment inflicted for the protraction of my confession, he sent for my mistress and me.

When we entered Miss Juliette's parlour, he said to Blanche: "I have just seen in the list of correction, that Adelina has been punished. I had forgotten to give her a note of justification. This punishment is unjust and I ask Juliette to give her the Blue Ribbon as a recompense. Thus she'll reward her for her submission and resignation. I take her under my protection and I exact that she is annoyed by nobody."

"I shall be all the more happy about the distinction of which she is the object," replied Blanche, "from the fact that, though I seemed vexed with her, she never bore me a grudge, but on the contrary worked with more zeal and willingness than ever."

Juliette kissed me on both cheeks and tied a blue ribbon with a star around my neck.

This reward gave me a right to go to bed at eleven o'clock, if I liked, and to get up at eight, and to circulate freely in the whole house, except during the hours of school and study in the evening.

Thus proclaimed, the Chaplain's protection made me in a certain measure a little favourite sultana and I should henceforth be able to intercede in favour of my friends.

That morning he was content to kiss my forehead and I returned to the study with Blanche, who published the nature of my reward to my schoolfellows, and the success I had had with the Chaplain.

In spite of Isabelle's low spirits in my presence, Angèle did not share her anger, but granted me her most devoted friendship as before.

I very often passed my recreation time with my charming friend, who, when she saw my senses roused, took me to her little room and gratified my desires as best she could, lest I should allow myself to commit some indiscreet act.

Such performances were as sure as one's daily bread, it is true; and there was nothing of the unlooked for in it, but I longed for Isabelle just because she insulted me most cruelly whenever we happened to be alone. Not once did she spare me when we met.

Putting a finger in her mouth she cried: "Dirty beast! Sucker! Oh, she runs after men!"

This vexed and irritated me. I dared not speak of it to anybody. The Blue Ribbon allowed me to get into the secret of this constant fury.

Having suffered her punishment, Marie Rougemont resumed her seat at my side. One day she whispered in a low voice: "During the recreations you may take one of your friends with you everywhere. Take me to the dormitory that we may repeat the little thing the same as the other night, you know! We shan't be punished."

I consented, but before tucking up my petticoats to abandon my bottom to my companion's fancies, I told her of her great friend's abominable conduct.

"Well," said she, "if you had answered by calling her a Sodomite, an *enculée*; if you had thrown yourself upon her and had drubbed her soundly, she would love you and lick you from head to foot. That's her way. She wants romances with the pupils and at the least adventure gets vexed and tortures them by her nonsense; but she takes care never to be surprised. That's the way she behaved to Athénaïs, who gave her a regular drubbing; since then they get on well with one another. You are strong and though she probably will be nervous, don't spare her on the first opportunity you can get at her.

"Sodomite and *enculée*? What's the meaning of that?"

"Don't you know? Those are the words for receiving a man's prick in one's bumhole."

"Prick?"

"Dear me, the instrument, yes? Isabelle is the favourite of Mr. Grandin, who always inserts it into her bum, from what I have heard the elder girls say."

"Thank you. Now you may amuse yourself with my arse as much as you like."

The little minx had her revenge, and in spite of my petticoats and my drawers, belaboured me so long and so well in the right place, round the orifice, that she made me spend twice. She accomplished her pleasure by giving me six or seven slaps on my fundament which set fire to my buttocks and which I only put up with, in order that she might avenge herself for those she had endured for my sake.

The school time passed as usual, but at the end of the lesson Blanche received a note from Miss Robert, after the reading of which she said: "Go to the chapel during the recreation, Adelina; the Reverend Father expects you."

I guessed that he was about to make use of his privileges and, if I had been in doubt, the looks of my schoolfellows and their remarks would have enlightened me.

"Look here," whispered one, "before you do what he demands, ask him to give a nocturnal feast in honour of you. We dance and amuse ourselves, you know. You cannot imagine how funny it is."

"Propose an inspection of the dormitories," recommended another. "Afterwards, we have great fun and enjoy ourselves immensely."

And a third: "Don't be timid. He has always a great liking for fresh girls, you know. What ever you wish, tell it him and you'll see that they will throw the house out of the window for your sake. He is one of the most important shareholders of the school and it is he who decides whether pupils are to be admitted or not."

The Chaplain awaited me in the sacristy and took me into the little boudoir where I had amused myself with Isabelle.

A dainty repast was served on a small table and he invited me to eat and drink.

While satisfying my appetite I saw a thousand burning flames sparkle in his eyes. His hand rested on my knees.

Crunching one cake after another, I smiled and let him do as he liked.

His hand slipped under my petticoats and he tickled me between the thighs. After that, he tucked up my petticoats, and setting me on his knees, placed his big instrument, his prick, between my buttocks, in the furrow you know, and encircling me with his arms, clasping his hands over my belly, he lifted me from time to time by the vigour of his member which insisted upon standing straight up.

When I had appeased my hunger, he said: "My little favourite, my own darling! Before we abandon ourselves to luscious, sensual pleasures, I want to do something for you. Give an order and it shall be executed."

"Then it is really true that I am your little sultana?"

"Who said so, darling?"

"One of my friends."

"Her name?"

"Why? You would perhaps think of her, and I want to remain your little affectionate sultana."

He was charmed with my answer. He forced his tongue into my mouth and pressed me to his heart.

"You are a little minx! In spite of all their success, I don't think there is a single one here, who can cope with you."

"You say that because I am new to the office."

"What a coquette! She would damn me if it was not already done. Look here! What do you demand?"

"A nocturnal feast."

"That has been suggested to you. I should like something which would please you in particular."

"But I'll enjoy a nocturnal feast!"

"Well, be it so. Let us fix upon the end of this week, on Saturday, for instance, then they can repose themselves on Sunday. But now you must suck me a little. Afterwards I shall ask you to give yourself up to me as you did to the Abbé Dussal."

I trembled all over.

Sitting on his knees I felt his prick wander everywhere under my arse. When he transferred it from the furrow to under the buttocks, it seemed by the facility with which it pushed me from one side to the other, to be even bigger than it really was.

I threw my arms about his neck and said: "Yes, but perhaps you'll hurt me."

"Don't be afraid, darling! The human body is capable of being stretched, and even if it hurts you a little at first, that will soon be over. I'll tongue you well and before approaching you I shall apply plenty of saliva to the bumhole; then he'll enter as if it was the purest butter."

He did not undress me. He unhooked my bodice,

manipulated and titillated my bubbies, and afterwards I knelt down between his legs to suck his prick.

He did not spin out this pleasure. He laid me down on the divan and with his tongue between my buttocks sucked the orifice well and hurriedly, exciting and stirring it to frenzy.

He slavered about and around it and when he had besmeared it well with his thick saliva (like the boa smears its victim) he drew me between his thighs and made a first attack with his prick.

But he did not succeed.

Then he took the member in his hand and directed it towards the orifice. I lifted up my fundament to help him. All of a sudden the knob penetrated, but I could not help setting up a cry of pain. He hurt me so.

But now he was there at it, he did not mind.

He put his hand on my lips to suffocate my screams. I kissed and bit it, but my arse responded to the attack, the pain struggled with my voluptuous nature, his prick got farther in than in my mouth, and his liquor inundated my entrails and produced the effect of a wonderful balsam, which instantly healed my wound.

He had spent and spent in abundance.

He looked at me, satisfied and full of admiration. I strutted with pride.

I guessed that my ascendency over the senses of this authority of the house was secured and that a new era of felicity was beginning.

Indeed, he told me in confidence that I had acquired this power over this thoughts.

"My darling," said he, "you are but a child in years, and yet you are a woman. You combine in your person the grace of your mistresses and of all your companions. You have been found out and formed by my old friend Dussal. I won't be jealous; but look! The other gentlemen will certainly strive to take you from me. Remember, that I am the most powerful of all and that if you can refuse them or at least restrain yourself with them, in order to preserve yourself for my pleasure, you shall be more mistress in this house than the Misses Géraud themselves."

Only think of that, Paul, think of the sway your dear sister bears. Oh, why can I not ask him to let you come here; I should like you to partake of all my joy and felicity.

Being already a woman by all that I had learned, I replied to this fit of the Chaplain in the only way possible: I pressed my lips to his and I was happy enough to wring a deep sigh from him.

"I don't want you to miss your study, my dear; so do not tempt me to begin again. I'll see you very often. Dress quickly and get you gone, you little devil!"

More news before long, my dear brother!

Your sister,

Adelina

III
From the same to the same

How proud I was, when I thought of my prerogative, you can scarcely imagine!

Only one fear made me uneasy; I was afraid of exciting the jealousy of the Misses Géraud and my mistresses. There was, however, no help for it.

In the evening, when the junior classes had retired, Juliette and Fanny joined the pupils who had remained behind, and taking me aside into a corner, they entered into conversation with me.

"Your education and your instruction, my dear child,"

said Juliette, "leave nothing to be desired. Your tutor has been very successful and has pushed you far. You are in advance of all your classmates and in addition to this your physical growth has been proportional. You would, therefore, belong to our superior class, if our rules did not require in the most absolute manner that the pupils of this form have entered their sixteenth year, and that there is a place vacant by the departure of another pupil. At present the number is full. Awaiting the possibility of your removal to the first class, we shall consider you belonging to a class intermediate. The Chaplain's protection manifested so plainly (a thing he never did before) puts you in a well-nigh exceptional situation. Your admission into the confraternity of Red Girls will be indispensable; we shall speak about that another day. We rely upon your discretion and good behaviour, so that you don't make discontented or hurt the feelings of your companions and your mistresses. Can we trust you?"

"Yes, my dear mistress. I desire no better than to love and obey you."

She kissed me, and Fanny added: "Not too much at a time, my dear! In a few weeks we shall celebrate your triumph in our turn."

I went to bed at nine o'clock and got up at seven as I did not wish to abuse my prerogative.

The opportunity which I had decided to look for, in order to put an end to Isabelle's irritating persecution, presented itself this morning.

When I was on the point of leaving the dormitory, I found myself face to face with Isabelle in the doorway.

For a minute we looked at each other from head to foot; then assuming her evil look, she said: "Hem! You think, perhaps, that your blue ribbon and the protection of the man you suck will stop me! But you are wrong, you are! You are a dirty whore, I say, a real cod chewer!"

The crudity of these words, which I had never heard before, but of which I understood the signification, made me furious with anger. I rushed upon her, pulled her by the ear and gave her two or three boxes on her head. Before she had recovered from her surprise at this sudden attack, I had pushed her towards a bed, tucked up her petticoats and from above her drawers gave her several cuffs with my flat hand. I struck as hard as I could.

"Ah," I cried, "you call me a dirty whore, do you! You use such nasty words, that if the Principals knew about it, you would be severely punished. Come along! Defend yourself, if you are so strong. There is a cuff for your dirty bottom, you *enculée*, you Sodomite! How could I ever caress it! If you insult me once again I shall not hesitate to tell Miss Juliette, and that will make matters very bad for you, I assure you."

At first she tried to kick, but my anger increased my strength and she was small in spite of her vigourous strength. Besides, feeling herself guilty, she did not defend herself as well as she might have done.

By flogging her I had torn her drawers and perceiving her naked skin I got wicked and pinched her furiously.

Her cry of pain was stifled by her sobs and she declared herself beaten.

Lying with all my weight on her loins I flogged her cruelly, but at length her tears interrupted my blows.

"Forgive me, forgive me," she whispered. "I will never tease you again. I was vexed for two reasons: first because I wanted to be your best friend and secondly because I was looking for the Chaplain's protection myself. Don't strike again, please! I am your senior. Look here, you haughty girl, let us make friends again."

Being distrustful I kept myself on the defensive. She folded her hands and looked at me with loving eyes; then she continued: "Look, Adelina. Let us make it up! Is it not thanks to my rendezvous, that you've obtained all this success? Be a good girl! I'll be your sweetheart, as we agreed, if you like."

She was really charming, the darling creature, in her beseeching attitude! Yet I resisted her attentions and, remembering Marie's advice, I said: "I desire nothing more than to forget; but you have insulted me so far that I must have a convincing proof of the warm friendship you offer me."

"Whatever you ordain me to do, I accept in advance."

I reflected a few moments and then said: "Look here! I was going to the privy, when I met you. Wait outside the door till I have finished, then I'll call you, and you shall wipe my bottom. Afterwards you shall wash it and lick it. I might exact that you did so after you had used the paper."

"If we are surprised we shall be flogged with the rod, and even the Chaplain's protection cannot preserve you from that."

"So much the worse! That's what I want and nothing else."

"Be it so, I consent."

The little closet was not far away. She was upon the watch, and as soon as I had finished she took the paper and wiped between the buttocks I presented her.

She laughed, saying: "There are no traces left; it's not a difficult stroke of work. Besides, your arse is so pretty and so white that all reluctance must disappear. I'll lick it instantly, if you wish me to do so."

"No, only after the water," said I.

We returned to the dormitory; she washed me, dressed and perfumed the hair, and while I leant the upper part of my body against the bed, she slipped her little head through the opening of my drawers and returned a hundred fold the caresses I had showered upon her during the famous rendezvous at the chapel.

The final rapture was not allowed. It was time to go to the class, and we parted, promising one another frequent meetings.

Alas! We were both to atone for my foolish demand.

The little Lisa Carrin had heard our discussion.

She told everything to Miss Robert, who came to verify the denunciation of the child. She was present at the end of our debate.

Miss Robert made a report to Miss Géraud.

After school I was summoned to Miss Juliette.

Very annoyed at the whole thing, she addressed me as follows:

"Adelina, you have, in concert with Isabelle, committed one of the greatest faults our school ever heard of. I should prefer to screen both of you from a punishment which will not fail to provoke the anger of two of the persons whose support is valuable to me, but this is impossible because of the pupil who saw you. I am sorry, angry, and, I confess, afraid of the consequences of your thoughtlessness. I don't understand where you have heard words like those you employed. I know that Isabelle is of vehement, sometimes even dangerous, disposition, a being corrupted from the very beginning, whom we have had great difficulty in disciplining. But you, Adelina, who are brought up in an honest, innocent family, where have you learned the words they repeated to me? One of your schoolfellows has prompted you, I suppose, and I won't urge you to denounce her. Don't employ such words in the future! Believe me, my child, pleasure is something so beautiful, so charming, that we must never tarnish it by gross language.

This accident brings upon you flagellation with the rod, forfeiture of the Blue Ribbon, privation of recreations for a fortnight, separation from your companions for a month, and, in addition, daily subjects to do. The Chaplain will never authorize such severity. On account of his protection I'll evade the difficulty. With exception of the school time you shall have no intercourse with your companions; you will be brought to my rooms, where they will suppose you to be punished. This shall last till the day of the flagellation, which you cannot escape. Afterwards I'll remit all punishments on account of the nocturnal feast you have asked for, and your schoolfellows can't speak of injustice, while they will be indebted to you for their pleasure. I beseech you, in your own interest as well as in ours, to avoid such excesses, or take your precautions so as to create no suspicion among the pupils. Your mistresses will shut their eyes."

Moved by this kind demonstration I swore never to begin again.

If I was terrified at the thought of the flogging they had promised my poor posteriors, I was on the other hand extremely glad to substantiate the importance I had gained by the Chaplain's protection.

He was my acknowledged lover and I had great influence with him.

I had a proof of that the same evening.

About half past six I was engaged in doing my exercise in Miss Fanny's drawing room, when the Chaplain entered in great emotion. He brought me a beautiful comfit-box.

He knew of the whole affair and he told me that he had been so sorry, that he would not have my pretty buttocks spoiled, that he had threatened never to enter the house again if they did not profit by the nocturnal feast and immediately remit this as well as all the other punishments.

"Has Miss Fanny consented?" asked I.

"No," said he. "She pretends it is necessary to set an example. I don't care a pin for the example. When I happen to have found such a delicate, such a charming little sweetheart, I will not allow her to be flogged with the rod."

"Don't trouble. I defer to their judgment. A little one has seen what we ought to have concealed. The torture won't be long; I submit to it and if you have any regard for your little friend, don't be angry with my dear mistresses."

"She is perfect. Oh, my child, you don't know the effect of those lashes! For more than twenty-four hours your injured posterior will be unfit for all pleasure!

"If you are pleased to make use of it before or after, you'll find it quite willing."

He kissed my eyes and replied: "I must keep within compass. I must not tire it with my big prick! I love you, my darling, indeed, I do!"

He conducted my hand to his dreadful tool and I frigged it (I get conversant, you see) according to his most explicit directions.

He would not even permit me to suck it; he tried to govern his senses to make me understand the ascendency he gave me authority to exercise over him.

Fanny surprised us in this attitude. Addressing the Chaplain, she said: "You'll spoil the dear child, I fear!"

"No, my dear friend. She has just asked me not to screen her from the flagellation. The school has made a precious acquisition in her person."

"That you have taken notice of her," replied Fanny, "is a proof that she is of eminent worth."

The Chaplain's prick strutted hard as iron between my fingers; a violent desire came over me.

I had a splendid idea.

Fanny was within my reach; I seized her by the

75

petticoats, tucked up her clothes in front and pushed her towards the Chaplain's thighs.

Was this what she had hoped for? She was instantly astride over him and her misty looks expressed her gratitude.

The Chaplain did not hesitate. He put in his member, and wishing to enjoy the sight, I squatted down behind Fanny and lifted up her petticoats. I perceived the prick working in and out of her cunt.

I added from beneath my tonguings, now to Fanny's arse, now to the Chaplain's testicles and very soon they began to tremble in an agony of delight.

Lying under them, my clothes tucked up, I frigged my clitoris and at the very moment they died away in ecstasies, I discharged.

His sensual desires gratified, the Chaplain, before going away, returned to the subject that preoccupied him.

"I want her to be avenged," said he. "Four of the little ones shall pay for the denunciation."

"Forgiveness," murmured I.

"No, my dear, no mercy! Your arse will be flogged with the rod, four of the little ones shall be whipped."

"The pretext is easily found," interrupted Fanny. "The little one was at fault. We cannot punish her for having revealed the scene she witnessed; but we shall inflict a punishment for the moral responsibility on a third part of her class."

These few lines, my own Paul, give you an idea of the position I am about to obtain in the school. In the bottom of my heart I pique myself on it.

You may expect some wonderful news one of these days.

Your loving sister,

Adelina

IV
From the same to the same

Oh, what a pain! I never imagined it would hurt like that!

The Chaplain was not present at the execution. Mr. Grandin, Isabelle's protector, had, though he was very pale, the courage to stay to the last.

Considering the gravity of our fault, the series of chastisements began with Isabelle and me.

We arrived before the Council and the united classes with out nightgowns tucked up behind and fastened to our shoulders with pins so as to exhibit our posteriors and legs in all their plumpness; our dishevelled hair hung down in front on each side of the face.

They had exempted us from carrying the chamber-pot, but we had several slips of paper in the hand. Thus we arrived in the middle of the hall. Miss Nannette ordered us to imitate the action of wiping one another, which excited our companions' hilarity and our confusion.

Taking the paper with which I had wiped Isabelle's posteriors, Nannette passed it over my face, saying: "Kiss what you like, Miss Dirty, there's no accounting for taste. So much the worse for you if you have a mind for what is coarse and nasty."

I burst into tears, humiliated and greatly moved, while she went through the same scene with Isabelle.

My friend was in possession of the most perfect coolness.

She kissed the paper without reserve; then, pointing at the pupils of the lower class, she said: "One must always be sure to amuse the children."

There were two trapezes over our heads.

We were attached to them by our arms but so as to be able to seize the bar with the hands.

I soon learned why.

77

For the flagellation my bottom fell to the lot of Miss Nannette, that of Isabelle to Miss Robert.

The two rods were raised at the same instant, whistled in the air, and fell heavily on our buttocks.

I screamed aloud, thrust myself forward and set the trapeze a-going; I seized instinctively the bar and ran with it.

Another blow made me rise, that is to say made me withdraw my legs and follow the swinging movements of the trapeze.

When I returned I received a third blow and by this time I presented so ridiculous a spectacle that the little ones writhed with laughter while the elder girls and the pupils of the middle class cried out: "Mercy on Adelina!"

When the little ones began to laugh Miss Juliette rose and mercilessly picked out four of them. They were brought out of the rank in order to be whipped for their scandalous hilarity.

I was not quite aware of what was going on.

Dragged along by the trapeze, I contracted my legs in the hope of avoiding the cuts, and whenever I returned the rod fell on my buttocks and the thick part of my thighs, compelling me to set up one loud cry after another.

The punishment accomplished, we were released and brought out. I was still crying.

Blanche led me along to the dormitory, anointed my poor fundament with cold cream, and advised me to rest. When I was in bed, she left me.

The four children paid for the denunciation. They were thoroughly whipped and being anything but stupid they guessed the motive of their punishment—though nobody ever told them the real cause—and for some time they bore a grudge to little Lisa Carrin.

I had a fever the whole day and did not get up till next morning.

The bright sunshine dissipated in the incubus; nothing was left but satisfaction at having delivered my dear mistresses from an anxiety.

Angèle and Marie, who in their turn received each twelve lashes for our sake, did not cry. Angèle said: "My dear Adelina, this is the second time I have suffered flagellation on your account; I am not vexed, yet I must inform you that a third execution will break our tie of friendship. I shall be very sorry if this happens; therefore, try to avoid it."

My great friend and I began to be very intimate together.

Having learned from Isabelle what was her taste, I unbuttoned her bodice as soon as we were alone, took out her breasts and sucked the nipples. She grew quite frantic with passion.

Another time she asked me to flog her, at first softly, then harder and harder. This excited her and she always finished by spending.

On her side she was very fond of me and knowing that I loved to be caressed *en minette*, that is to say, to be licked between the thighs, she very often gratified me in this way.

The announcement of the nocturnal feast, which was arranged for the following Saturday, and the remission of all the punishments, effaced the bad impression of this day, which by the way, brought me another success.

I perceived during the recreation the tender regards which Nannette sent me from her velvet eyes and I smiled to encourage her.

She hesitated for a whole day, but next evening, when her pupils were asleep, she went downstairs, entered the

parlour, where I had remained behind—I had regained the
Blue Ribbon, of course—and made me a sign.

I joined her with all possible speed and on the landing,
she said: "Will you be so kind as to keep me company for
some minutes in my room. I should be so happy."

"Indeed, Nannette?"

"Little minx, come quick!"

We entered noiselessly, letting down the curtain in the
doorway, which separated her room from the dormitory.

Sitting on her bed and looking admiringly at me, she
said: "Life is a strange thing. I have been a form-mistress in
this boarding school for more than three years; I have seen
new pupils enter, not many it is true, for the recruiting is
but in slow progress, being contingent on definite and
irrevocable conditions. But nobody ever made an effect like
you. The last to enter was Lénore Grécoeur; she has gone
her even pace without exciting more fancies than any of the
elder pupils. It is true that they generally belong to the
junior class. Yet, we have had one great girl, Diane de
Verson. It went on as quietly as possible. But you, you
bring perturbation into all the classes and to all your
mistresses."

"But you are the first who ever thought of me."

"And Blanche?"

"Only once, after my first punishment."

"And Fanny, and Juliette, and Élise?"

"No, no, no!"

"It is rumoured that everybody runs after you
stealthily."

"I hear about it for the first time."

I was standing before her. She kept her legs swinging to
and fro and by this movement her petticoats by and by got
up above her knees. I guessed that she desired my caresses,

on the spur of the moment it seemed to her that it would be an agony of delight to feel my little phiz ravage her buttocks and thighs, and being already clever at the art of exciting the sense, I amused myself with waiting till her lasciviousness had prompted her to commit some excess.

She sighed and grew agitated. Her petticoats rose higher and higher; I perceived the white, appetizing skin of her thighs. I did not stir, having taken it into my head to talk.

"This boarding school is a terrestrial paradise," murmured I.

"Oh yes," replied she, "and neither the pupils nor the mistresses ever forget it."

"What a grief it must be to leave it!"

"Nobody ever leaves it but to marry or to enter on an independent situation, which permits them to return."

"One can return?"

"Yes, on great festival days and for the Red Offices."

"The Red Offices?"

"You will know what that means, when you belong to the confraternity of Red Girls. I am sure the Chaplain will want you to be a member."

She made up her mind to take my hand, drew me between her legs, and conducted my fingers to her quim.

"Look," said I, tickling her lightly, "you have flogged me as best you could with the rod. What would you say if I frowned at you now?"

"Naughty girl! You can't find it in your heart."

Pressing down my arm she took hold of the upper part of my body, leaned on my head and threw her legs about my neck. My lips were glued to her rosy, shivering little slit; she trembled all over.

What a charming sight, my dear Paul, you ought to have felt her pretty thighs caress your cheeks, her convex, silken belly touch your forehead, her curly hair tickle your nose and your lips, and at the same time have what I had, the view of her rounding buttocks below.

Nannette did not complain of my tonguings, and spent twice on my face.

Then interrupting my caresses, she said: "I am selfish. Get in bed, and in my turn I'll make you discharge; afterwards I shall ask you to regale my buttocks and I'll do whatever you like in return."

Ah, what a dexterity in tonguing. She was much more skillful than Angèle, the only person who had done *minette* to me at the boarding school.

Her tongue titillated me everywhere; her hands lifted my buttocks; her lips burnt as she sucked in the hair of my mount, which has become both longer and thicker, since I left Chartres. I spent all on a sudden, dying away just as she tried to nibble my slit with her teeth.

Then she presented me her arse, the beauty of which I had admired in the presence of Blanche, Fanny, and Marie. It was like a dream!

She raised it on a level with my face, approached, retired and flattened it on the bed or against my face; she wriggled in all directions, all the while keeping hold of my tongue, jammed in between her buttocks.

I doted upon these caresses and devoured her arse so fervently with my kisses and suckings, that she placed her hand on my head, pressed it with a sudden clasp and discharged, shaking so violently that my nose at each movement ran down the furrow from the beginning of her loins to between the thighs where it was moistened by her liquor.

We had not undressed.

Lying together in the bed, my hand in hers, she asked: "Did you enjoy it, darling?"

"Oh, yes, and you?"

"Like a baby! Do you think I am well made?"

"You are as beautiful as an angel."

"You flatterer! Do you think me as pretty as the others?"

"As yet I have scarcely looked at anybody."

"And Fanny and Blanche and Isabelle, my rival as regards the arse; and Angèle and all those of whom I don't know. How many do you want, you epicure?"

"I want to see them all."

"You are frank, you little rogue. Rome was not built in a day, you know. By help of time and method your desire will be gratified I dare say. Look here, darling, shall we agree to meet often?"

"Oh, yes! I like you very much. I must, however, tell you, that I have promised to be the sweetheart of Isabelle."

"The intriguer! She makes her way everywhere. Well, don't refuse her; she can have but intermittent relations with you and she is very changeable. Consent without any underthought to my proposal."

"With all my heart, Nannette! But then you must promise not to strike so hard, when I deserve the flagellation."

"Did you not ask to be punished yourself! Look, is Isabelle's arse prettier than mine?"

I laughed and replied: "Indeed, they are almost alike as regards form and qualities."

"Oh, then you make a comparison, while licking?"

"You ask my opinion; how can I give you an answer without recalling it to mind!"

"Fie upon the logic, ma'am. Do you pretend to become a schoolmistress!"

"I should not regret it if it were at a school like this."

And in addition to all this, my dear, no end of kisses,

tonguings and suckings! Time ran fast; we parted to go
soundly to sleep and recover new strength.

Good night, my own brother!

I suck it for thee!

Yours,

Adelina

V
From the same to the same

The friend who advised me to ask for a nocturnal feast
was no fool. What a day and what a night!

I fancied that I saw you there, my dear Paul, and thought
of all the follies you would have committed!

Perhaps you would have taken ill, so it is better that your
pretty little muzzle did not enjoy the great triumphs of
which I dreamt!

From the early morning modification of all rules: We got
up one hour and a half later than usual; our toilet
accomplished, we awaited the visit of Dr. Bérnard de
Charvey, who would call to examine the state of health of
each pupil and to decide whether they were able to support
the pleasure—and the jollity. We were stark naked, having
only put on our stockings and boots. Miss Blanche gave us
notice, when she called us, by clapping her hands, saying:
"Medical visit!"

My companions knew what this meant; Marie Rougemont put me up to the thing.

The doctor went successively behind all the curtains; we
received him standing before our beds.

When my turn came, he examined me from head to foot,
fingered every spot of my body, placed his ear against my
breast and back and belly, telling me to cough. Satisfied

with the result of his examination, he said: "Robust constitution, you'll go far, my pretty one."

He put a finger between my thighs, tried to force it in, while I at a significant look plunged my hand into his breeches.

I touched another edition of the male weapon, a short, but very, very, big prick, much bigger than the Chaplain's.

He bent me backwards and approached it to my cunt—for a minute I thought he was going to take my virginity.

He stopped short. Belly to belly we kissed one another and he whispered: "I forgot myself; I have not yet finished my inspection. But we shall meet another day, my darling."

One thing puzzled me.

As soon as the doctor left a *chambrette*, its owner entered Miss Blanche's room, from which she did not return, till she had been replaced by another pupil.

I entered in my turn and got the explanation of the mystery.

Blanche was lying on her belly in the same attire as we, abandoning her arse to Marie's skillful tonguings (*feuilles de rose*).

My companion retired unwillingly, and raising her head, which she kept resting on her arms, Blanche said: "Come, Adelina, give me a big kiss. There, suck my nipples. All that is perfumed, ready for all kinds of folly. Your body is in a perfect state, too. The doctor's report will affirm it, no doubt. Now, my darling, a caress on my buttocks and then return to your companions to dress and go down to the school room. This first caress from your form-mistress forebodes the pleasures of the nocturnal feast."

On Blanche's arse I recalled to mind some of the skillful suckings I had executed on Isabelle and Nannette. She trembled and whispered: "You have made progress since you were flogged. That will do, leave me. We must not protract the *séance*."

I opened her furrow far apart with both my hands, and my tongue, pointed as much as possible, fluttered around her bumhole.

"Oh, dear me! No! Stop! Get off! Don't make me spend, I say. You expose me to being guilty of a fault; to everything there is a season and a time to every purpose, you know."

I interrupted my caresses and gave her, laughing, a vigorous slap which rang in the whole dormitory. Then I ran away, while she gracefully held up her forefinger at me.

The dormitory was in uproar. The first who had been examined lay in state instead of dressing, and the others wandered from bed to bed.

Marie, who was kneeling before her curtain had, indeed, a fervent *clientèle* awaiting there to get their arse licked by her.

One after another presented her fundament, opening her buttocks wide with both hands; one after another approached her furrow to Marie's face and she swiftly executed a dozen speedy suckings with her tongue.

When I arrived, there were three of them left who with beaming eyes stretched themselves over one another's backs, whispering to her who gave up her arse to Marie's caresses: "That will do. Be quick! The rest of us will have no time."

The activity of her tongue was accelerated and each had her allowance of *feuilles de rose*.

Happily all severity was suspended that day. Blanche guessed what was going on, I suppose, and let us dress at our ease.

The afternoon school was advanced and at half past five

we gathered in the dining room to lunch. We were to sup at nine after the dance.

Lunch over, we went upstairs to dress.

Oh, my dear Paul, nothing was neglected!

I looked charming in my white dress, cut out to a point in front. It was the *chef d'oeuvre* of a clever dressmaker, a former pupil, who was now established, thanks to the protection of our Council. All the middle class was dressed in the same fashion and we wore no drawers, an important detail, you'll acknowledge! Our skirts reached to the ankles and if we happened to lift them up, one could admire our very long black silk stockings.

At seven o'clock we entered the apartment of the Misses Géraud.

I shall never forget the charming sight of the three rooms opening out of one another, splendidly lighted and pouring fire into our veins by all that we saw in them.

Juliette and Fanny were dressed one in black, the other in blue velvet; their bodices were cut very low and left their breasts almost quite free; their arms were naked and a spray of diamonds adorned their hair. They received us as the ladies of the house at the upper end of the first room.

Blanche was dressed in green silk, and Lucienne in lilac satin. Both dresses were as low-bodiced as the principal's and the skirts were very prettily slashed on one side, showing cloudy muslin undergarments, red stockings and their naked haunches. Nannette appeared in black male attire with white tie and so did Miss Robert and some of the senior girls, among whom was Angèle.

Georgette Pascal, the only one who wore a fancy-dress, was a soubrette Louis XV, a charming little rogue who roused a thousand wild desires by her funny manners.

But worst of all and the most extravagant were the little

ones. They appeared in their bare shifts with a blue or rose-coloured sash, their arms, shoulders, bosoms, legs and arses were quite naked; they seemed all very graceful in spite of the slender form of their yet undeveloped limbs. This apology for a dress was completed by a pair of white slippers, flowers on their hair and a bow on each shoulder.

And all these little vivacious creatures moved about, wriggling their arses to the right and to the left, enjoying themselves, patting one another, yet never overstepping the bounds of liberty and yielding obedience to a mere look from Nannette.

I observed some distinctions in the general ensemble of dress.

The Red Girls wore at their girdle a red velvet bow. On the hind part of my white skirt was attached a bouquet of violets and Isabelle, Berthe Litton and Georgette Pascal were adorned in the same manner.

It was a sign that the bearer was the favourite of some gentleman.

Indeed, Berthe was patronized by Mr. Callas and Georgette by the doctor.

We were all four kept back by Juliette, who conducted us to a retired boudoir, where we found the gentlemen.

"My friends," said she, "I bring you your houris. Before they are drawn into the whirl of the feast, I thought they ought to sacrifice a quarter of an hour to you. So have your will of them."

Isabelle, the boldest of us, jumped on the knees of Mr. Grandin and threw her arms about his neck.

I did not hesitate any longer but did the same with the Chaplain.

Georgette held out her hands to the doctor, who took her to his breast while Berthe waited until Mr. Callas approached her and gave her a kiss.

Juliette had left us.

"Gentlemen," said the doctor, "don't let us be selfish. We possess each of us a charming sultana, but let us give them permission to amuse themselves with their companions and let us bring them back to the parlours."

A voluptuous kiss and we returned.

They had begun to dance; Miss Robert was at the piano.

The couples whirled round. The little ones were not the least clever and they enjoyed themselves to their heart's content.

Isabelle asked me to dance and I accepted, though her clandestine looks betrayed that she was meditating another wicked trick.

I soon got the proof that I was right. Twice she pinched me treacherously and when in the midst of the crowd, she whispered: "You are a nice sweetheart! I thought, indeed, that you would be more faithful than that! Since our punishment we have not met a single time and you have amused yourself with Nannette. She is not worth as much as I, I assure you. And moreover she is vexed with me, because I boxed the ears of her Camille Grandin. I don't care a pin!"

"Oh, Isabelle!"

"Don't bother me! Let me speak if you do not want me to say some nonsense in the presence of the whole society. I never mind what I say, you know. I learn all that from Camille and it amuses him that I use bawdy terms. A sweetheart of your kind is able to drive one mad with lust. I am very hot-tempered and I must be kept up or I get angry. If I did as I feel inclined, I would give you a sound drubbing and I have on my lips all kinds of filthy words. And yet, I have cleaned your bottom with my tongue!"

"You had washed it before you tongued it."

"I would nevertheless have done it directly, I proposed to

do so. After what we agreed in the chapel I thought we should have got on with one another; but you don't seem to care. After all it may be that you prefer an arse like Fanny's or that of Athénais! If so, you are not difficult to please. A pretty little bum, very round, not too fat, well-marked—in short, you are perhaps like the men who prefer them very plump, round like a full moon! Look here, why don't you answer me, you strumpet?"

"Isabelle, I implore you not to employ such words."

"All right! It's because of you that they have torn my buttocks with the scourge and I have in all been punished twice on your account. Indeed, as yet we have not been fortunate in our intrigues."

"It is not my fault."

"I have a right to be vexed! You never put yourself in my way, and opportunities do not always present themselves. The night you went upstairs with Nannette, I reckoned upon your understanding my oglings! Pooh! My lady was dreaming and a single sign from that blessed Nannette made her run away. Oh, you dirty beast!"

It amused me to see her so vexed, the more so because she waltzed very well and I could splendidly keep time with her, though our bodies were glued to one another.

I gave myself up to her vigorous pressures and suffered myself to be carried off in her arms while my breath mingled with hers.

"Oh, you have finished defending yourself, eh? You accept my injuries, little Miss Nothing; you would give yourself up to anybody but to your friend Isabelle. Indeed, you begin to behave like a harlot."

"If you continue speaking like that, I'll go away from you."

"I've too good a hold on you, this time it's my turn to tame you, I think. I press you in a close embrace, my voice tickles you as well as my fingers would tickle your cunt and my nonsense excites you. I know it is so, because you smile, you naughty girl! You forget that I am your elder and that I have more experience in those things than you."

She led me as she pleased and the surroundings furnished matter for the conversation.

Sometimes the waltz diminished in strength or even quite ceased, to permit some of the couples to take rest or to change partners; the most eager stopped in cadence and then went on again; those roused a roar of applause. We were among them.

On the armchairs or on the sofas the gentlemen amused themselves with one another. Two of the youngest pupils were standing on the Chaplain's knee and let him enviously titillate now their front, now their back sides.

I did not reply to Isabelle's last thrust. Glueing her lips to mine, she continued: "Do you deserve the honey of my caresses, you dirty beast! You who called me names the other day; you who have had both your brother and the Chaplain. When you will blame the others, don't taunt them with your own actions."

"You call me a suckeress, but have you never sucked a prick yourself, eh?"

She smiled and replied: "If I did so, it was to please my protector. And you do it because you like it."

"Every taste is allowed."

"I won't quarrel with you about that. I am offended at your indifference and if you prefer Nannette, it is not necessary that we should be sweethearts."

"I prefer nobody, but I like to amuse myself."

"Why did you not call me?"

"And you?"

The waltz was over and we parted without having contracted a new alliance. Angèle, as nice-looking as possible in her male attire, engaged me for the next dance.

Being an excellent pianist, Isabelle was asked to play the piano in order that the mistresses might get their part of the pleasure.

She retired, sending me a clandestine look ominous of some future attack.

Angèle encircled me with her arms, kissed me and said: "Take heed against Isabelle, my darling, she sticks and it is difficult to get rid of her."

But what was the matter? At the upper end of the room they crowded together, animated, agitated, on fire!

A thing that anywhere else would have compromised the discipline of the school!

Élise Robert and Nannette, bearing the train of Juliette had, by tucking up her clothes, uncovered her buttocks and all the little hussies were now kneeling behind her, kissing her arse, encircling it with their slender arms, giving themselves up in caresses, which seemed to fascinate our grand principal.

One replaced another and afterwards they ran about the room, shooting forward their little round buttocks, which some of the elder pupils from time to time gave a light slap.

Isabelle started a mazurka; Angèle grasped me in her arms and off we went!

It is late, my darling; I'll put off the continuation of my recital of our nocturnal feast till my next letter.

Your *Adelina*, who kisses and bites you.

VI
From the same to the same

After this mazurka Nannette carried me off for another waltz, and said: "I'll lay a wager, that you had a scene with Isabelle?"

"Oh, no!" replied I.

"You are afraid of compromising her? Don't fear. I'll do her no harm. One cannot control one's fancies and in spite of her malicious and changeable character she is a nice girl. Personal affections do not exclude voluptuous desires. Blanche told me you had given her the dildo. Will you give it to me too?"

"To be sure, whenever you like!"

"Even if Isabelle put a spoke in our wheel?"

"She is but a pupil and you are a mistress."

"That's no reason, my dear. Pleasure alone ought to inspire your heart!"

"I should like it; have I not already enjoyed your body?"

"That's better. You've a great deal of natural discretion. Act on the spur of your personal fancies, and your mistresses and your companions will not complain."

"An idea has puzzled me very much for a while."

"Which, please?"

"Are not the little ones dangerous?"

"No, they are well trained, managed, and overlooked, and they know they will lose the opportunity of amusing themselves if they tell tales. Three-fourths of them do not leave the school during the holidays, because their parents are afraid that they might recommence the fault for which they were brought here. Besides generally all the pupils, whether belonging to the superior, middle, or lower class, wish but to remain within our walls.

"It cannot be the Misses Géraud who founded the school; they are too young, are they not?"

"They have only had it for five years. They bought it of the Chaplain's sister who retired because she grew too excited; at that time Miss Juliette had the management of the upper class."

"I thought as much."

Suddenly my look became haggard and following the direction of my eyes, Nannette could not help smiling.

"Are you jealous?" whispered she.

"No; oh, no! But I think that is going it rather far."

I had just seen that Lisa Carrin was kneeling between the Chaplain's thighs with his prick in her mouth. The sentimental Lucienne d'Herbollieu was standing beside him, her skirt tucked up, abandoning herself to his titillations, while he with half-shut eyes and thick lips panted like a man who is on the point of spending.

At this moment the evolution of the waltz carried me towards the piano and my eyes met Isabelle's. She indicated with an ironical look the group of the Chaplain and his two accomplices. I confess that in spite of the answer I had given Nannette I was overcome with a fit of jealousy.

The dance was almost over. This waltz terminated the first part of the feast. It was time to take supper. Encouraged by the mistresses, excesses were going on everywhere.

Before the scenes in view Nannette gave me some details concerning the mysteries of the house.

Fanny Géraud was very fond of women and her greatest passion, her dearest, most tender friend, her particular sweetheart, happened to be Élise Robert, whose violent lesbian temper excited and stirred her. The two women often slept together, living like husband and wife, and from time to time they added a zest to their pleasure by taking one or two of the little ones between them.

Juliette had as a set-off a real lover. She received frequent visits from the husband of an ancient pupil who had been her favourite when she had the management of the upper class; their relations had continued at the festivals of the Red Girls.

Lucienne d'Herbollieu, the sentimental beauty, was of a very lascivious temper and sought especially sexual intercourse with Nannette; but she did not neglect some of her pupils, amongst whom were mentioned Isabelle and Josepha de Brougier.

As the name of Isabelle was brought upon the tapis again, Nannette did not fail to cry: "You see, one is sure to hit upon her everywhere!"

The last measures of the waltz were played and she ceased her communications.

I examined swiftly the whole of the room; the amorous fever was perceptible in every corner. Everybody spoke in a low voice; no noise was heard and people gathered in groups to gratify their sensual lust.

Élise Robert had Juliette on her knees, their tongues were billing and cooing in each other's mouths. Perceiving Marie Rougemont occupied with Anne Flavart's bum, Juliette cried: "Marie, I offer you mine, as you are so fond of them."

She stretched herself across Élise Robert's thighs, tucking up her petticoats behind, and happy, proud of the permission, Marie showered down her most graceful caresses upon Juliette's pretty arse.

As Élise was sitting on a couch Blanche got up beside her and standing before her presented her cunt, wanting *des minettes*.

Clémentine de Burcof, a slender blonde of eleven, rather
tall for her age, looking almost naked in her apology for a
dress, went from group to group, titillating, getting titillated, bold, shameless, tucking up rebellious skirts, asking
now here, now there, for a suckeress, somebody fond of
caressing arses. Extravagant and foolish as she was, she ran
away as soon as someone was going to satisfy her to address
somebody else.

Angèle, my great friend, was together with Georgette
Pascal; while hugging one another their hands had strayed
down between each other's thighs.

If Isabelle had shown me the Chaplain, Lisa Carrin and
Lucienne d'Herbollieu in a scoffing manner, I might have
taken my revenge by calling her attention to Mr.Grandin,
who was occupied with a pupil of my class, Marguerite
Dechelles, a brunette of thirteen, tall, vigorous, rather
stout, but very graceful, very womanlike, with well-
developed buttocks, of which he seemed very fond, no
doubt by way of contrast to Isabelle's.

Fanny clapped her hands and everything ceased as by
enchantment.

Supper was ready.

The meal was served in the refectory. Besides the usual
three lengthwise tables there was a fourth placed crosswise
so as to preside over the other three. This was the table of
honour.

As the nocturnal feast was given at my request I took my
seat there between the Chaplain and Angèle.

This part of the feast was very delightful.

The tables being splendidly laid with flowers, cakes,
confectionery, and no end of wax candles increased the
general joy.

Some of the pupils waited at table under the direction of
Georgette. The attendance left nothing to be desired.

"Well, my little friend," said the Chaplain. "And you for whom this surplus of life is glittering, are you enjoying yourself?"

"I have danced a great deal," answered I, bluntly.

He took my chin in his hand and asked: "There are no painful thoughts concealed behind this pretty forehead, I hope?"

Indeed, I must confess that I was crestfallen.

"You little flirt," added he, in a low voice. "Tonight I leave you to your pleasures; don't refuse yourself the gratification of your fancies; the advantages of this feast, a real Saturnalia, I assure you, consist in the fact that the pupils turn mistresses. We shall meet later on to fix our divine relations, my dear."

On sitting down to supper Miss Juliette had made the following speech: "My dear children! We only wish you joy and happiness. I recommend you to avoid noisy fun and cries, so that we may not regret either our kindness or the confidence we have in your discretion. After supper every caprice is allowed. You go to bed noiselessly and without disorder at midnight when your mistresses give the signal. Now, help yourself to what is on the table like reasonable people and you will encourage us to repeat these feasts."

"Our mistresses for ever," was the general cry from all the tables.

"Hush, hush, children, no hubbub—please!"

The description of the meal can have no charm for you, my dear Paul; so I'll skip it. It lasted for more than an hour. Afterwards we scattered to all sides. The flower of the party remained in the ballroom.

I, too, went there. Marie, my best classmate, said in the name of several of her companions:

"My dear Adelina, we are indebted to you for this feast. Be so kind as to amuse yourself with us for some minutes in order that we may give you a proof of our sincere friendship. Command and we'll give you the caresses you ask! Would you like me to begin by your arse, eh?"

"All of you? But that will take you the whole night."

"Oh, no, heyday! The funny story," cried Lénore. "Let us go upstairs; it will go on swimmingly in the dormitory."

No sooner said than done.

In an instant the petticoats were tucked up and I could admire a charming collection of thighs and buttocks. Squatting down behind me, Marie took possession of mine.

I abandoned myself to the fun as in a delirium. I fingered the first, the second, the third, and so on. I received and gave caresses in abundance and growing more and more agitated by the game, we knelt down behind each other, kissing and licking each others' arse and cunt.

The creaking of steps on the staircase dispersed us like a brood of startled ducklings.

The grown-up people had left the drawing room; that is to say that the pupils, great and small—not all, however, for some of them had been carried away to the rooms reserved to the Board of Directors—used their own discretion.

We thought of nothing but amatory delights.

Isabelle was spending with upturned eyes under the *minettes* of Berthe Litton.

Two of the little ones, Pauline de Merbef and Clémentine de Burcof, both precocious and premature children, were wriggling ostentatiously in the midst of the room, surrounded by an inciting crowd. They formed the figure of 69. Angèle, one of the spectators, directed the combat of the two children who, enjoying their mutual caresses, only stopped to throw out a casual remark to the by-standers:

"Show how you are made, eh?" The pupil thus addressed instantly tucked up her clothes.

Athénais! Caffarel came up to me, saying, "Will you accompany me?"

I was on the point of accepting when Isabelle, disengaging herself from Berthe, rushed forward and interposed in the most bullying manner: "I have asked her before you."

"How could I know that?" replied Athénaïs. "I won't give way."

"Adelina is my sweetheart and in this capacity she belongs to me rather than to any body else."

"Is it true, Adelina?" interrogated Athénaïs.

"Yes," replied I. "Isabelle and I have come to an agreement; but I don't refuse you for that."

"But I want you to refuse," cried Isabelle harshly.

"Oh, what manners," said Athénaïs. "She does not belong to you and before all she is the favourite of the Chaplain and he will be vexed if you monopolize her like that."

"Don't meddle in the affairs of others. I do what I like; I'll show you, if you run after her."

I did not know where to look during this discussion. I found my friends and myself very ridiculous.

Isabelle seized me by the arm and dragged me along with her to the dormitory. She had no room of her own.

"Why did you not refuse?" said she.

"I did not know that the fact of my being your sweetheart excluded me from all other pleasures."

"Even if I beseech you to do so?"

"You can't be in earnest. Why not enjoy all kinds of amatory delights?"

"Because I want your caresses and you won't give me them."

"Now we are together, let us profit by the occasion."

"You are enervated; you will not caress me well."

"You are a funny creature. Don't let us chat, but act!"

"You know what I like?"

"Yes, you told me the first time. You like to get your arse tongued; Marie has given you a taste for that. Indeed, you do not merit that I lavish my caresses upon it after what you have done. Nevertheless, it is so sweet, so pretty, so excitable, that I am dying to tongue it."

She jumped on the bed, tucked up her petticoats and showed me the subject.

The heat emanating from it penetrated all my pores and I determined to excel myself in caressing it.

I got more and more experience at this game. After the respects I had rendered the arse of Nannette and the caresses I had received myself from Marie and others I began to appreciate the voluptuous charm of these pretty twins and I really believe that I was on the point of catching my friend's passion.

When I had Isabelle's pretty dumplings before my eyes and heard her whisper in a low voice that she was longing for my ardent endearments, I contemplated them for a minute and then began to caress them with the palm of my hand. My heart leaped within me.

Swinging her leg to and fro, Isabelle held her peace. Her arse described a serpentine winding following the movements of her leg.

She was lying on her left side and presented me three-fourths of her bottom.

She understood by the pressure of my hand and my pushing her a little more forward that I wanted to approach my face to this blooming plumpness, and she turned round on her belly.

Then my tongue fluttered over her arse from the loins to the thighs, my fingers slipped to her clitoris; I frigged her, kissed her, sucked her, excited to the utmost by the contortions of her bottom, her back, her legs and arms, by the enervated, soft movements of her whole body, disporting itself in a thousand feverish attitudes. Then the passionate girl all on a sudden turned round and flattened her arse on my face to make me feel its active throbbing, while she frigged herself.

Tearing herself out of my arms and gliding to the bed's head, she then said: "Come along, try to catch it."

I threw once more my contracted arms around her and got her within reach. She crouched into a ball and my tongue penetrated like the point of a bayonet into the orifice, causing her to jump and leap with lust.

She spent three times during this violent attack and I discharged almost incessantly.

She was as charming as possible, fondled me in her arms, took me to her heart and whispered: "With whom else could you enjoy such felicity, Adelina? Both you and I are very lustful; we shall get on capitally together. Come, I'll tongue you in my turn and you will see that I am as quick to deliver caresses as to receive them. My kisses will dry you, for you are quite wet, and afterwards you'll love but me. Promise, that you will not do it with Athénaïs. I can't bear her. Promise, do!"

"If I promise about Athénaïs, you will demand the same respecting the others, and when I take it into my head that I will have some voluptuous enjoyment I shall be obliged to ask your permission. No, to that I cannot consent."

"Only as regards Athénaïs!"

"And Nannette?"

"Oh, you are the first to mention her! Yes, as regards Nannette too."

"No, that I cannot promise. I like Nannette."

"More than you like me?"

"No, but she is a form-mistress. I find her charms to my taste and I won't allow you to forbid me the enjoyment of them."

"Look here, do it secretly. What one does not know, causes no woe!"

"One would say you are mad at times."

"Perhaps! I know it. At present I want to keep your caresses for myself because they produce a greater effect than all the others. You have seen how passionate I am; I can't control my feelings. In spite of my affection for you I am sure to do you some harm if I learn that you enjoy yourself elsewhere, when you have but to speak to have all your whims satisfied with me."

She was enchanting! She played with my lips and my whole body; she overwhelmed me with caresses, imbibed my soul with her kisses and her suckings and I was on the point of endorsing all her tyrannical demands.

What can the scenes that were accomplished to the right and to the left be to you? The clock struck twelve and everybody retired to the dormitories or their private rooms; the light was put out, calm reigned everywhere and we went to sleep with feverish hearts and slept till a late hour on Sunday morning.

Now I am acclimatized, my love! A thousand kisses from

Your sister,

Adelina

END OF BOOK ONE

Book Two

Chapter Four
The Red Offices

I
From Adelina to Paul

Can I be sure that you do not forget me in the big English capital, my dear brother? It seems a century since we parted and several long weeks have passed since I wrote my last letter.

My looks are improving and my adventures continue, only interrupted by great felicity and a few corrections.

There are good and bad points in the flagellation. You have never tried it, darling! I think you miss a pleasure as well from an active as from a passive point of view.

To restore the equilibrium of our minds an extraordinary

severity was exercised for several days after the nocturnal feast. Thus the novelty of independence was stifled. The number of compositions was increased; the exercises that fatigue the body were multiplied; strengthening, but soporiferous, meals were wisely served out and all these things helped us to recover in a few days the strength we had spent during the nocturnal orgy.

Impossible for the little ones to err. The surveillance was uninterrupted night and day.

The senior pupils and those of the middle class felt the effect in proportion.

Everyone did her best to submit to this regime in order to ob'ain other favours, and punishments were rare.

The fixed period during which the Blue Ribbon was worn had expired and I was again subject to the daily discipline.

Blanche told me that if I placed myself beyond my classmates, I should certainly rouse their jealousy, which would cause me much trouble.

The necessity of going to bed at half past eight did not trouble me except that it prevented me from meeting Isabelle. ring the few evenings which I passed after the feast

During the few evenings which I passed after the feast I had seized several opportunities of having an interview with my hot-tempered friend, and according as she abandoned her cunt and her arse to my violent caresses I got foolishly fond of her. The passion by which she was governed had passed into my veins and my blood boiled at the mere thought of the bliss she gave me by the skillful movements of her arse.

The wicked girl watched joyfully the progress she made on my senses, and, as Angèle had predicted, she literally pinned me to her petticoats.

All day, during the recreations, when I was playing with my companions, I thought of her secretly, and if she smiled at me in a certain way, a lascivious, mysterious smile, accompanied by a movement of her hand or her hips to attract my attention to her waist or her back, it would seem that her flesh called mine right through the clothes and a torrent of fire thrilled me through and through.

During the time of my permission to go to bed late, our intrigue became more and more intimate and with the exception of my encounters with the Chaplain, I did not think of other sensual pleasures.

It was in vain that Nannette tried to get hold of me again; I avoided her under pretext of fatigue, or feigned not to understand her.

One day, shortly after the nocturnal feast, the Chaplain took me to the little boudoir behind the sacristy.

He complimented me as usual on my good behaviour and my discretion, and assured me that he was extremely fond of my little person.

He kissed my lips, set me on his knee and beseeched me to give him my whole confidence, saying that he wished me happiness not only during my sojourn at the boarding school but in after years too, when I had married.

"Tell me whatever you desire, my darling, your old friend will be happy to meet your slightest wish."

A hearty kiss was my thanks for these kind words. Then he stripped me stark naked, taking off even my shoes and stockings.

He placed me on the divan and told me to assume different poses, while he undressed himself.

He made me lie down on my back, my head on a level with my body, my legs drawn up and crossed; then I had to stretch and cross my arms over my head, while my legs were well spread; then he made me turn towards the wall, leaning upon one arm while my free hand caressed the furrow between my buttocks and at last I turned on all fours, the arse well up and the head level with the ground.

By this time he had finished undressing and stood in his turn stark naked before the divan; he slipped his head under my belly, got it between my thighs, lifted one of my legs and licked my cunt, my buttocks and my bumhole.

I moved about, as I had seen Isabelle do; he got on fire, devoured me with *feuilles de rose*, and tried to penetrate my maidenhead with his finger.

I sighed. I was dying to get hold of his tool.

He guessed as much, and getting under me placed himself in the charming attitude of 69. Thus I was enabled to suck him.

The more I saw of his prick, the bigger it seemed to be. I grew, however, accustomed to it, and when his hand pressed my buttocks, I understood that he wanted to bottom-fuck me. I arranged myself in consequence and pushed my bottom towards his thighs; he turned briskly, jumped on my back and penetrated into my bumhole with violent leaps and bounds, which soon made us spend together in ecstasy.

He overwhelmed me with caresses and then told me he was going away for several days on urgent business. But on his return, he said, we should keep up continual intercourse.

Bereft of the Chaplain's society and the favours attached to the Blue Ribbon, and subjected to the general rules, I began my exclusive attachment to Isabelle.

She expected me, no doubt, at this moment, as my soul and my senses only lived upon our luscious combats.

She showed alternately periods of indifference and periods of passion, which tormented me cruelly.

The heartless girl confirmed her dominion over me and laughed at my distress.

When she had not spoken to me the whole day, I wrote

her the most ardent letters; she locked herself up in the most absolute dumbness and disappeared during the recreations; I did not know where to find her.

She exasperated my senses; I interested myself in nothing but her charms; the most foolish visions flitted before my eyes; day and night I dreamt of her lustful body, her arse rocking and fleeing before my lips.

Then she would come back, fix a rendezvous, and in an hour of ecstasy overwhelm me with such intoxicating caresses that everything else faded and I saw nothing but her.

I stuck to her petticoats and conscious of her ascendency, she resolved to carry things to extremities.

For a whole week she refused me all contact; then, one evening during the recreation she said: "You would eat my buttocks if I gave them up to you too often, and I want to preserve them. I am proud of their attractions. You are always running after me, and you prevent me from satisfying my little friend Marie and the others who want them. I am very fond of you, because you are my chosen sweetheart, but we must conciliate our fancies. Look here! At present I have taken a fancy to the little Clémentine, and on Saturday night, at midnight, when everybody is asleep, I steal away to her dormitory. I awake her if she be asleep and we enjoy ourselves. This is the day. I'll take you with me when I pass, and we'll have a three-handed game."

"Oh, Isabelle, what a gross fault you propose to me."

"We shall not run a greater risk or rather we don't risk as much as when I licked your bum that first time. Besides I want this proof of the strength of your desires."

Saying so she put on so determined and wicked an air, that I became afraid we should fall out, and I gave way.

By committing this fault I should offend Nannette, towards whom I bore an intense interest in spite of my amorous neglect; trying to argue with Isabelle, I murmured: "The pleasure we'll get, will have no charm; we'll be afraid of being surprised and Clémentine's bedstead will be too narrow."

"Danger stimulates voluptuousness. As for the narrowness of the bed, we'll arrange for that. Yes or no? If you don't accept, it is all over with our friendship, you know!"

"I am afraid!" replied I.

I was not only anxious about Nannette but about Clémentine too—the impudent little blonde from the nocturnal feast, you know—before whose persecutions I, though her senior, had been obliged to flee on more than one occasion.

She had been at the boarding shool for a year and she was more than precocious. She had been debauched by her mother's maid, and it was rumoured that the husband of this creature had been on the point of violating her. On her crying out for help, people came running and the foul plot was discovered; the two servants were sent away lest the story should get wind and the child was confided to the Misses Géraud. Her temperament was promising. The examination of the doctor being favourable, a hygienic treatment had been fixed in order to increase her growth and a mean degree of pleasure was allowed in order to have a hold on her. She figured among the favourites of Fanny and Élise, and belonged to the Red Girls.

She enjoyed great liberty in the house, though she was rather indifferent at school.

Her parents required but a plain instruction and she was overcharged neither with exercises nor with lessons. She was rather developed in social accomplishments for which she was gifted; she was especially clever at music and drawing.

Four or five days after the feast, believing myself alone at the further end of the garden, I had just squatted down on the lawn to piss when I discovered Clémentine, who proposed to drink my urine as it purled out.

"You dirty little beast," cried I, "are you not ashamed to ask such things?"

"Ashamed? Why, if I like it! May I?"

I had finished and replied: "If you repeat your request, I'll inform your mistress and she will punish you."

"You'll be a babbler and I'll do you all the harm I can. You were flogged with the rod through Lisa Carrin and you are welcome to it again."

"You are a shameless little blackguard and to show you how little I care for your menaces I'll go and tell Miss Nannette everything this very instant."

"Go! You'll regret it soon enough."

She walked slowly after me and saw that I did not address her mistress.

Another day, during the recreation, she entered the library at the same time as I. All on a sudden she stooped, and slipped her head under my petticoats.

Before I had recovered from my surprise, she set her teeth in my buttocks and then rose, saying: "That's to teach you not to take notice of me!"

I was content to pull her ears and to reply: "We'll talk over that matter when you are a little taller."

"People older than you do not refuse me!"

"I don't care to imitate them."

"But I want you to care and you will care!"

Finally a third time she came to my bed at night. I was on the point of falling asleep, when I saw the little dogmatist pull my curtain.

She approached my bed's head, kissed and sucked the tip of my nose, and whispered: "You won't send me away, eh?"

I trembled for fear of being surprised; I gave her a push and replied in a low voice: "Be off now, or I'll call Miss Blanche!"

She contracted her lips, put her tongue out at me, and answered: "You are a dirty beast, a jade! But I have not given myself trouble for nothing. I assure you, I'll find a more amiable and attractive companion than you."

She left me. I heard her call Marie.

Less saucy and half asleep, the latter asked: "What do you want, Clémentine?"

"Hush! To amuse myself, of course. You are willing, are you not?"

Was she not, Marie! An arse and a willing heart offered themselves! Not the least noise betrayed what was going on behind the curtains. Next morning Marie told me in confidence that she had retained the little one for more than an hour. I had fallen asleep again.

Afterwards, if her eyes spoke, Clémentine feigned to treat me with indifference and disdain, and now Isabelle demanded that I pay the little devil a visit. I had promised to do so.

I am sure, my dear, that *you* would not be at a loss about that; you would rush headlong into the adventure, I dare say!

But there are prejudices of which one is not the master. I have come to the knowledge of that.

A hearty kiss from

Yours,

Adelina

II
From the same to the same

Everybody was asleep; the most profound silence surrounded us, when I saw Isabelle pull my curtain, and with a finger on her lips heard her whisper:

"My love, my love! You were waiting for me. Come quick!"

My hands got under her nightgown; she smiled and allowed me to titillate her cunt, but added: "Let us be quick. We shall be better down there; Nannette is a heavier sleeper than Blanche."

I got cautiously out of my bed and followed her. My dormitory opened upon that of the junior class by a doorway, only covered by a curtain.

The Chinese lanterns gave but a dull light; everything favoured our adventure. We glided like shadows.

Clémentine slept in the fourth bed of the second row. The minx awaited our arrival stark naked.

"Well," said she scarcely audibly, "there you are, at last!"

Jumping out of bed like a monkey and slipping her head under my nightgown, she applied her lips to my cunt and kept it in close embrace for a minute.

Isabelle pressed my hands, approached her lips to mine and sent my soul into ecstasies by changing some drops of her saliva for mine.

Clémentine gathered up my gown in front, did the same to Isabelle and then pushed our bellies towards each other with her hands. Afterwards she squatted down under us and placed one of her hands on my buttocks; we remained motionless in this attitude, while she breathed on our cunts and we kissed and tongued each other's lips.

I forgot myself in heavenly delight. All of a sudden I felt my thighs get wet.

Astonished at this I stretched out my hand and found the explanation.

Less decent than I, Isabelle had pissed on the face and shoulders of Clémentine who, frigging her little cunt like a madwoman, swallowed a good deal of it.

Hugging me in her arms to prevent me from escaping, my sweetheart suddenly spouted out the jet of her piss over my quim and my belly.

There is nothing more infectious than great filthiness. I took example by the others, and consented in my turn to this disgusting scene. I poured my urine, which she longed to taste, straight into Clémentine's face, and to my great astonishment Isabelle arranged her belly under my thighs in order to be irrigated by it.

Clémentine was jubilant; the sensual rapture mounted into my head. Kissing my lips, Isabelle whispered: "Wait, stop! Piss into the furrow of my bum."

Turning briskly, she placed her bottom between my thighs, and, meeting her wish, I poured out the rest of my piss on her arse. Below, Clémentine received this new kind of douche, almost beside herself with delight: she glued her lips to my friend's arse and licked it in order to dry it, as she said.

We had finished with this loathsomeness.

I made sure that it was premeditated when I discovered a towel on the carpet, placed there by the sly Clémentine to prevent the water from wetting the floor.

The dirty little creature's body did not tempt me very much in spite of my ebullition.

Isabelle was less particular; she licked the shoulders and face of this filthy cherub, pretending that it redoubled her sensual desires.

We cleaned ourselves carefully and every trace of the pissing scene was effaced.

Stark naked, we abandoned ourselves to our mutual passions.

Isabelle liked Clémentine because of the horrors she would suggest, because of the flavour of her yet undeveloped body, and she showered upon me the lasciviousness she imbibed, caressing me in the most frantic manner. Afterwards she returned to the child and enjoyed herself in good earnest: she distorted and hugged her in her arms, she covered her with her own body, kissed and tongued her; they struggled in raging lubricity, encouraging each other by filthy words and ridiculous proposals.

The little one contested with her great friend.

She sought the marks of her teeth in my buttocks, a wound which was scarcely healed, and finding it, she whispered: "She would not permit me to suck her pipi in the garden and today she consented; she sent me away when I came to her at night, and Marie sucked my bum so soundly that I thought she was going to swallow it with all its contents. I say, Isabelle, your friend is but poorly trained!"

"There are not many gluttons like you, you little ninny; all people cannot understand that you are so coarse and filthy at such an early age. I like it, but Adelina is a sentimentalist."

"Tut, tut! my dear. A sentimentalist, a person who thinks of nothing but sucking bums, your bum; I wonder where she hides her sentimentalism. Nurse always said that people who were afraid of pimento had better not sit down to supper. She called pimento what you designate horrors and what you nevertheless do. She pushed her cunt-curls laughingly into my mouth, recommending me to smell well at the sap of her husband, who had just had her."

"She has given you a careful education, the baggage!"

"So I believe! I know everything, and you may be sure I was delighted to enter this box. Indeed, that was a happy day! Well, Adelina, do I not lick you as well as Isabelle and your other friends?"

Kneeling behind me, the little rogue honoured my buttocks with her most skillful tonguings, while she kept the head of Isabelle, who was lying on the carpet, between her thighs to receive her *minettes* and *feuilles de rose*.

I stretched my arms, I gave myself up, I listened, I awaited my chance to get possession of Isabelle, whose sinuous body presented itself before my eyes.

"You little tattler," said the latter, "tell Adelina how the entrance of your palace was on the point of being forced."

"Oh, that's a foolish story! Men must be deucedly dirty to run after such impossibilities. I amused myself with Annette, my mother's maid, and at the same time my nurse, to whom I was confided incessantly. She was a vigorous creature, who had always some immoderate desire hidden under her petticoats. She brought me to her room and there she rolled upon her bed without saying a word, kicking till she had tucked up all her clothes and I could see her thick, black hair, her white arse, and her plump thighs which opened and shut with loud smacks. I dared not speak, nor ask questions. I looked at her and finished by liking it. Having kicked about sufficiently long, she flung herself on all fours, poising on her arms, her petticoats over her head, and her arse came and went, while she whispered to herself words among which I distinguished, 'Oh my love, my love! That's nice. Oh, I spend! Yes, put it further in, still further, my love! Again!' I was dying to approach and touch her body, but I was afraid she would jump over me. She was obliged to call me to her, before I could make up my mind to go near. I perceived her head through her

116

wide-spread legs; she smiled to me and invited me to kiss
her by slipping my head between her thighs. Well, I seized
the opportunity, and no mistake! Oh, the first time that
filthiness makes itself the master of your soul, how you
enjoy it! From that day she taught me the most delicious
things in the world and she was exceedingly exciting. Her
husband Joseph fucked her often, and she had the mania to
make me smell the odour of man. One day when we had
locked ourselves up together, Joseph arrived unexpectedly
and surprised us. He did not say a word, but undressed,
seized me, in the twinkling of an eye, by the leg, pulled me
down under him and placed his big member between my
thighs. At first I thought it was some new fun, and I only
laughed. Annette scolded her husband, boxed his ears,
abused him like a pick-pocket, and tried to pull me from
under him; but he held me fast, pressed me harder and
harder till I got frightened. His tool hurt my cunt and I
wanted to escape. He lay heavily upon my belly and I
thought he was going to burst my thighs. I set up one cry
after another. Somebody heard it and came running and
there was a great uproar. I need not say more. I acted the
part of a poor innocent, the servants were sent away, and I
was locked up here. Now I was so much the wiser."

She told her story with self-possession and imperturbable
coolness and never neglected her handplay nor her tonguing
and all the while made numerous kicks at the buttocks and
legs of Isabelle, who was convulsed with laughter at the
looks, gestures, and fooleries with which the child accentu-
ated certain passages of her tale.

Seeing this radiant little blonde, nobody would have
thought of the depravity which she displayed. Compared to
Isabelle, who was renowned for her vice, her depravity took
such proportions, that I asked myself, how far will she go?

She loved naked bodies and she inebriated herself in

filthiness with Isabelle, explaining the coarse words which they delighted to repeat.

At length my friend abandoned herself to my caresses, and Clémentine said to her: "You are heartless to have let ler languish so long. If somebody wants to suck me, I consent immediately, and if they want *me* to suck, no matter where and whom, I'm always ready."

We soon formed the most charming triangle: my head rested on the thighs of Isabelle who transferred my caresses to the posteriors of Clémentine; the latter favoured me with her most skillful tonguings.

We were fortunate enough to regain our beds without any accident; but the next morning some trifles betrayed us.

Having abused the time, I slept so soundly next morning at the reveille, that they were obliged to shake me to make me jump out of bed. And what a face I had!

In the dormitory of the little ones Clémentine never thought of the linen employed as a sponge for our urine; she went to sleep leaving it where it was and when her neighbour got up she cried out that something was smelling.

Nannette came to see what it was, discovered the linen, and examined Clémentine, who replied that she had not taken care and probably, being half asleep, she had pissed on it.

This incongruous explanation did not satisfy her mistress. In the bathroom our guilt was substantiated.

Some dirty water, and one of my pocket handkerchiefs smelling of urine, with which I had wiped Clémentine's shoulders, became presumptive evidences. These facts were put together; Clémentine and I were accused of nocturnal intercourse. Not knowing what fib to tell, I defended myself badly, and Isabelle was the only one who escaped.

We were condemned to flagellation with the scourge till blood was shed.

The cruel Nannette, whom I had neglected of late, took a dreadful revenge. She was charged with my punishment and she brandished the scourge with all her might, thrashing my poor arse so severely that it soon was covered with bleeding scars.

Clémentine and I, both stark naked, endured the punishment at the same time.

Neither of us cried.

I wept silently at first; afterwards I fell into ecstasies. A strange, pleasing sensation tickled my epidermis, and as the scourge hit again and again, as my body got aflame, it thrilled me through. A shivering ran down my spine; the pain was assuaged and replaced by a sharp, violent sensation; I almost fainted away in luscious rapture.

To that my imagination lent a helping hand.

According to Angèle's and Isabelle's advice I had promised myself to seek the sensual pleasure of the flagellation and I succeeded.

Clémentine presented, by the distortion of her arse under the cuts of the scourge, such a seductive spectacle, that as some of my friends told me afterwards, our mistresses frigged themselves from above their petticoats.

The devil of a girl squeezed her buttocks together and when the blow hit, opened them suddenly, shivering all over and imitating the movements of a bird taking wing.

The climax of this affair was the punishment decreed by the Council on our mistresses for their defective surveillance.

Both were switched as common pupils by the superintendants Élise and Georgette. The execution took place directly after our punishment and in our presence.

We were down on our knees on each side, Clémentine beside Nannette, I beside Blanche. Their petticoats were pinned on their shoulders, their hands and legs were tied together and six times the switch was raised against their buttocks.

As mistresses they could not revolt, but their visages and the contraction of their limbs pleaded for them.

Besides that the chastisement in itself is very distressing when you occupy a public situation, the suffering is the same to everybody.

Blanche was very pale, and started at each cut she received from Georgette Pascal; her arse was marked off with red lines and her legs trembled. She tried to smile, but she bit her lips, which had grown quite thin. Her eyes gazed at random avoiding to fix themselves upon us, the only witnesses, as the execution was accomplished in private.

Nannette affected stoical firmness, and Élise Robert thrashed her soundly, while she as bold as brass slipped her left hand under her petticoats to frig her clitoris.

The buttocks of this sufferer, less full than those of Blanche, shivered and distorted, swaying to and fro. It was evident that Nannette knew the method, and that she desired the voluptuousness of flagellation.

When they had received their six cuts we dragged ourselves on our knees to their buttocks to kiss them and beseech our mistresses to forgive us, swearing never to do it again.

But another atonement was reserved for us.

Tied together, back to back, we saw all three classes file through, making game of us.

Isabelle who had got well out of the adventure flung out the most painful affront. When passing, she cried to me: "Debaucher of babies! Take care not to run after great people next time. There's something in store for you!"

These were the consequences of the punishment: My friendship with Angèle, who was not flogged this time, was broken; my relations with my mistress were extended; I received a severe rebuke from the Misses Géraud who accused me of hypocrisy, unable to understand my foolish escapade with a child, a Red Girl, it is true, but as such doubly inviolable.

All is not rose-coloured in this life although it is a life of pleasure; that we know to our cost, my dear Paul!

A thousand kisses from,

Adelina

III
From the same to the same

The Chaplain's return freed me from the disgrace in which I lived.

After all I did not care very much; I worked as best I could, did my exercises, and tried to divert myself otherwise.

I comprehended the danger of communicating with Isabelle, who treated me with great indifference, while she manifested an ardent friendship for Eulalie Pierre of my class, in order to tease me; this pupil was not on very good terms with me.

Isabelle's behaviour irritated me the more because, knowing me separated from Angèle and cognizant of the desire with which Isabelle inspired me, Marie had proposed that we should exchange our great friend on condition that

I favoured as much as possible the pleasures of which she was fond.

Isabelle refused, pretending that she could learn no more from an intrigue with me, and that she preferred to keep Marie.

My friendship fell upon Ève Philippe, the pretty blonde whom I had flogged at the first *séance*.

We had been friends for some time, and she assured me that she was delighted at my choice.

Ève Philippe had not a room of her own as Angèle had, and this circumstance, coupled with the exercises, which kept me away from my companions for a whole fortnight, delayed the definite adjustment of our league. More serious than three-fourths of the pupils, Ève was what is called a book-worm, and she obtained so much praise on this account that she often boasted of it. In this mood she did not fear a discussion with Lucienne.

Thus she brought upon herself the punishment of which I had been the tool.

She had entered upon her seventeenth year and it was generally supposed that, her education accomplished, she would decide to stop at the school as third superintendant; this would render possible an improvement in the situation of the form-mistresses by exempting them from the surveillance in the school rooms and an augmentation of the number of pupils.

She had entered the school at the age of twelve years and six months for a business like ours. Later on both her father and mother died, leaving her a small fortune of £1600. A bachelor uncle had been appointed her guardian. He was a captain and, being at sea all the year round, was but too happy to leave Ève with the Misses Géraud. Her brother, her senior by two years, often called to see her.

Forgive me all these particulars, my darling, but I want

you to like my new friend. Speaking of her brother we came to speak of you; I need say no more.

As soon as he had returned, the Chaplain asked to see me, and he closely questioned me about the report of my late offence against the rules.

With him I was sincere; I confessed the whole truth, asking him not to recur again to this adventure which had caused me such hard requital. I told him about Isabelle's hateful behaviour, which did not surprise him, and I assured him that I bore no malice for the severity with which I had been treated.

He took me at once to Juliette.

The great principal frowned at me. She was without mercy when the little ones were misled beyond the authorised occasions.

She understood that there was danger in it, and she would unmercifully have sacrificed three of the middle or even three pupils of the superior class for the violation of the dormitory of which I was accused.

The Chaplain began by saying that the question was not of a denunciation but of a confession, which he wanted to disclose to prevent the injustice from continuing.

Before revealing anything he asked her to pledge herself to forget and not to punish. Juliette promised and then she learned the real part I had performed that night in the bathroom.

She scolded me once more earnestly, because I had allowed myself to be beguiled, and then forgave me.

"Don't trouble yourself about it," said she. "Isabelle won't know that I am aware of her complicity. Don't attach yourself to this dangerous child. Alas! She is sure to make her way in the gallant world; she will probably be one of those who forget us in a few years. This oblivion is the best we can wish for from that kind of character."

"And if those ungrateful creatures speak?"

"Our public annotations will defend us. They are designated as hysterics, suffering from hallucinations. Nobody will doubt our good faith."

The Chaplain took occasion of this interview to ask for my admittance into the Red Girls.

"Let us wait till she has been in the house for six months; that will be soon enough."

"They have almost expired."

"Yes, but not yet; however, I promise you that she shall belong to the confraternity before the next Offices."

"That will do!"

I rejoined my schoolfellows during the recreations and having kissed Angèle who was now the great friend of one of my classmates, Louise Trossac, I went up to Ève who looked at me with her angelic sweet eyes. She took me in her arms and whispered: "Oh, we shall love each other dearly?"

"Oh, yes."

"You won't regret our friendship, I hope."

Nobody else seemed to take any notice of me and we began to chat.

However Isabelle was skulking about us, humming funny refrains.

The three united classes were playing at the long skipping rope.

Clémentine, being my junior and in consequence considered less culpable than I, had already resumed her place among her companions some days ago.

She was one of the most eager springers. Passing near me she threw herself about my neck and kissed me tenderly.

By the way of contrast Isabelle returned at this very moment, smiled scornfully, and said to Ève: "Your new

friend does not renounce her accomplices; you will derive
satisfaction from her friendship, I dare say."

"Everybody is not of your giddy disposition."

"Oh, giddy! What nonsense!"

"Whom did you not forsake?"

"You are all fools."

"Thank you for your kind judgment."

Isabelle shrugged her shoulders and ran after Eulalie who
from behind had blindfolded her eyes to make her guess by
whom she was addressed.

Looking hard at me she cried: "With this friend, at least,
one is not tempted to be giddy."

Eulalie Pierre, a brunette with very lively eyes, was
almost like a boy. It was impossible to say that she was not
well formed, but her square-built figure was destitute of the
pretty roundness for which the others were remarkable, her
straight hips did not develop themselves into plump and full
buttocks; her longish and lean-fleshed arse would have
fitted a young collegian better than a girl of thirteen. She
was tall, impudent, and imperious and she was conspicuous
by her long arms and legs, her rather narrow shoulders and
chest, and her hairless cunt. Dressed like a boy nobody
would have taken her for a girl.

She displeased me and it jarred upon me to see her so
free and easy with Isabelle.

The latter tried to catch her. They ran about the whole
court-yard; then Eulalie threw herself between Ève and me
and suffered herself to be taken by my late sweetheart who
laughingly struck her buttocks from above the petticoats.

"Adelina," said Eulalie, knocking against me as she rolled
about with Isabelle, "is it true, that you like people to piss
upon you?"

I blushed scarlet and stood disconcerted.

125

Isabelle kissed her, saying, "How stupid to mention such things."

"Where have you learned such terrible filthiness?"

"It is not necessary to learn it. One can smell such things near certain pupils."

I was on the point of getting angry. I had a mind to box her ears, but hesitated a minute to meditate; then I replied: "Some people lay at the doors of others their own faults and cultivating the society of certain friends, they grow as dirty as they are."

"Is that meant for a hint to me?" interposed Isabelle.

I replied to Eulalie, "Those the cap fits, let them wear it."

"Don't give yourself airs! Because you made a hit the very day you entered the school, you want everybody in the whole house to give way to your whims. I don't care a pin for your grand airs!"

"Adelina did not want to quarrel with either of you," said Eve. "I don't understand why you came to meddle with our conversation."

"Coo, my pretty turtle-doves, coo! You can't prevent us from saying what we think nor from putting pretentious fools out of doors."

This discussion was the opening of a series of teasings which influenced neither my character nor my immovability.

Isabelle almost hated me and altogether without reason. My class was divided in two camps, some of the pupils sided with Isabelle, who proclaimed war against me, the others took my part. This amused me immensely.

They served me some nasty tricks such as calling me Miss Urine, and placing a diminutive chamber pot containing a few drops of piss in my desk. I didn't care about that.

Isabelle wanted me to pay dearly for the passion I had for her body. This feeling did not diminish; I concealed it, that was all.

By this immovable calm I regained the affection of my mistresses.

One evening as I was about to go to bed Élise Robert came to fetch me. Fanny wanted me to keep her company.

This honour had not yet fallen to my lot and I was delighted.

Athénaïs Carrafel, Josèphine de Branzier, Mr. Camille Grandin and Dr. Bérnard de Charvey were there.

The Misses Géraud had each their set of rooms, allowing them to amuse themselves at pleasure without disturbing one another.

Fanny's drawing room, a beautiful place with fine looking-glasses, splended hangings, and numerous divans, was one sea of light.

On my entering with Élise, the voluptuous scenes were about to begin.

Athénaïs and Josèphine were sitting on the knees of the doctor, pulling his mustachioes and laughing as if they were mad; he had his arms around them and kissed their lips in turn.

Mr. Grandin, Isabelle's friend, had an intimate intercourse with Fanny, whose beaming eyes betrayed a burning sensual desire.

Fanny called me and said: "My dear, you'll soon begin your apprenticeship as a Red Girl; *en attendant*, you must show us that you are equally fond of all sensual pleasures. Don't refuse anything and nothing will be refused you. Do you understand?"

"That's to anticipate my most ardent desires."

"Is she not charming? I'll introduce you to a gentleman

who has heard of your talent for gamahuching. He asks to become acquainted with your art. Excel yourself and you will not regret it."

I was overcome with emotion. Mr. Grandin asked me to call him Camille, he led me to a divan, made me kneel between his legs and offered me his cock to suck.

It was a prick of the middle size, rather long and almost pointed at the nut. This kind of member is said to designate the best men.

Having taken off his breeches, Isabelle's protector showed me his belly covered with thick black hair and his big and heavy balls under which he placed my hands.

He pressed my head to invite me to take his tool between my lips and so I began to suck it, at first leniently, afterwards with more energy, while I kept his balls between my fingers as if I were milking.

I accelerated the movements, engulfed his prick to the hilt, and then let it out again; his leaps and bounds told me that I succeeded in my game.

I amused myself with keeping the nut on the edge of my lips for a moment; I clasped it between my teeth, looking maliciously into his face.

He gave me an affectionate tap on the cheek and whispered: "Go on, go on, you little coaxer. No pupil ever sucked me as well as you. I am tired of Isabelle and her fiddle-de-dee and I shall replace her by Athénaïs or Josèphine."

"But neither of them is in possession of the diabolic art of your favourite."

"Poo, they'll get it! Look at Athénaïs, look, if she does not know how to make herself appreciated."

With her petticoats over her arm and her body bending forward, Athénaïs abandoned her buttocks to Élise, who from time to time gave them an elegant little slap. They were standing before Fanny, who, her thighs in the air, was frigging her own clitoris.

"Besides," continued Camille, "if the nervous buttocks have their charm, the plump and full arses are even more attractive, when they wish for caresses. Fanny's arse is ten times more worthy, than Isabelle's. But, you little rogue, will you continue!"

Camille had recalled to my mind Fanny's plump posteriors and I immediately thought of comparing the satisfaction I should feel upon them to that I had felt with Isabelle.

How to manage it? I hurried on my sucking in order to get away and my haste betrayed me.

He guessed that I had some particular scheme in view and said,

"We shall meet again, my darling. Now I'll attack Athénaïs; go and satisfy your own desires, little one!"

The opportunity was better than I could have expected.

Lying at her whole length on the divan, Fanny, her hand on her mount, was contemplating the doctor who teased Joséphine while he smiled to Elise Robert and Athénaïs who were whipping each other.

I came secretly up to her, knelt down, and suddenly pressed my lips to her cunt.

She trembled all over and skipped on her buttocks which I managed to get into my hands. She entwined her arms round my neck and then threw herself backwards. I devoured her with *minettes*.

Oh, what a fire, what a passion, what a difference from all that I had ever caressed. I never should have imagined it and I asked myself how it was that I had not yet relished this rapture?

Fanny was indeed a staid woman in the flower of age, appreciating voluptuousness and inoculating you with it as by infection.

My lips inhaled the luscious draughts of her cunt. The perfume of her body excited my nerves, her sensuality roused my fever. My lips were glued to her quim, the point of my tongue dipped into her cunt and then ravaged the surroundings, multiplying itself in kisses and prolonged suckings.

By and by I lowered my head and my tongue caressed the root of her buttocks near the cunt. Fanny raised her legs more and more; her thighs and arse appeared at the end of the divine slit.

My breath became rattling. My dear mistress guessed at what mark I aimed; with a sudden movement she turned round and presented me her whole fundament.

It was no longer Isabelle's flexible nervous arse; it was not the long and rapid movements of the rotunda of my friend, trembling in licentious contortions; it was no longer the churlish domination of an arse, exacting the sacrifice of your whole body in the caresses, which it solicited. Yet it was a poem of grace, pliability, and majesty which stirred a thousand lascivious desires in your soul. The white full bottom, the deep, exciting furrow, the black hair below, all these exquisite rotundities before your eyes and the magnetical effluvia emanating from her body, all encouraged and stimulated your ardent love and proved its gratitude for the caresses you bestowed upon it. I had not seen it for ever so long, and I enjoyed it with all my heart, serving it with the same fiery caresses, that I formerly bestowed upon Isabelle's.

I felt it shiver and tremble. It raised and grew excited under my *feuilles de rose*. I imparted some of my passion to it and it began the movements of which I was so fond: it opened and closed spontaneously, contracted, expanded, displaying the most fantastic arabesques and in the midst of all this we died away in an agony of delight.

I triumphed and all the company crowded around to see the game, and congratulated me on my success.

Oh, my dear Paul, what a night of amatory delights and amatory combats! One lives it all over again in the description and we run the risk of knocking ourselves up. I should not like to hear that your voluptuous desires have enfeebled you.

A big kiss from your

Adelina

IV

From the same to the same

Fanny's little party fixed my final position in the house. On the other hand I entered my sixteenth year and by my age and my instruction I belonged to the superior class. I was to be promoted after the holidays.

I am terrified at my own bad temper. I have made friends with those who bore me a grudge; only Isabelle continues to hold me in contempt.

In a few days the Red Offices will be celebrated and I shall be admitted into the confraternity. Meanwhile I was initiated into a thousand little things, which quite enchanted me. There are all kinds of ceremonies which are at once amusing and charming.

The other day I assisted at a meeting of Red Girls at Juliette's.

At ten o'clock p.m. we were all assembled: the four gentlemen of the High Administerial Council; the mistresses, seven senior pupils, four of the middle class, and three little ones.

Our dress was most characteristic.

We wore nothing but a short black frock which stopped at the waist and left naked our belly, arse, legs, arms, and shoulders. On the head a hood, concealing the face with holes for the eyes and the mouth.

We made a very funny group!

All the little ones were placed in the middle; they were surrounded by the other ten pupils and the mistresses; the gentlemen placed themselves on the four sides of the circle.

I was the only one left outside. The doctor and the Chaplain took me to the women and told me to touch the buttocks and the quim of each of them.

And as I obeyed one placed his finger on my cunt, the other his on my bumhole.

Arrived before the three little ones I lay down at full length on the carpet and all the women turned their backs upon me.

Camille Grandin and Jules Callas squatted over me; one over my face to make me suck his prick, the other over my thighs to titillate my cunt with his cockey.

Afterwards I was asked to creep from one woman to another and to caress them.

Then we all rose. The little ones danced a sort of gavotte, while distorting their arses. Those of the middle class flogged four elder pupils while the other big girls and the mistresses gamahuched one another and I sucked the four men.

The whole resulted in a confused farandole, where the frocks whirled round and round, the eyes grew phosphorescent behind the holes of the hood, our bodies shivered from voluptuous desires, and we all flung ourselves down at sixes and sevens to gratify our lust as best we might.

What gave me the greatest satisfaction that night was when Fanny proposed to me to accompany her for a few minutes.

You will understand, I think, that I jumped at the offer.

She made me repeat the story of my escapade with Isabelle and Clémentine, and laughed heartily at the child's funny mania for drinking piss.

However it did not surprise her for, as she said, in the sensual rapture the most whimsical things are stimulants and while licking a cunt and feasting upon Love's liquor, one might very well in the agony of delight taste of the piss.

Listening to her words I thought of soliciting this favour. I dared not.

Indeed, I have made progress, my dear! But how can it be otherwise? The straining of the nerves urges one to the most violent means of appeasement.

She spoke in a low, soft voice! I was lying on her belly, in her arms, my lips glued to hers in ardent kisses and tonguings.

Her nipples pricked my bubbies, which are now well developed, and her tongue titillated my palate. She intoxicated me by her sweetness.

"That idea struck me once," said she. "It was when we began the direction of the school. Among the pupils of the superior class there was a golden-haired blonde between seventeen and eighteen years old, who was completing her education. She was delicate, tender, and sensitive, and she went into infinite ecstasies over a mere nothing. It seemed impossible that such a being could have material wants like other people and foolishly fond of her, as I was, I devoured her with *minettes* and *feuilles de rose*, which she returned with interest. The coquette scented her body with sweet perfumes which were consistent with her ideal beauty. A fixed idea took possession of my mind. I wanted her to piss into my mouth. In the midst of our delicious embraces I asked her to do so. She trembled like an aspen leaf and replied that it was impossible. 'Don't love me any more,' continued she sorrowfully, 'if you believe me to be unwilling. It is beyond my power. I don't understand why nature imposes such horrid things upon us and I should die with terror and shame, if I were obliged to obey.' I did not press her harder. I knew she was unable to tell a lie. I loved her like a deity and she left without having gratified my desire. I did not know that such whimsical lust was to be found in a boarding school."

I threw my arms about her neck and whispered: "Oh, I should like to taste yours!"

She shivered all over, took my head between her hands and replied: "Say that again, Adelina."

"Yes, I should like to taste it. Send me away, if I displease you."

"No, my darling, I am not displeased, but I cannot meet your wish. One is not the master of such things and Laurette's refusal bequeathed me a certain restraint in this function."

"I should have drunk it as milk from Heaven."

"Wicked girl, you must content yourself with our present pleasures. If one day I should feel inclined, I do not refuse definitively."

We had terminated our pleasures and I returned to the dormitory.

I was scarcely in bed when I saw the curtain move. I leaned on my elbow to see what was the cause, secretly hoping that it might be Fanny asking me to return. I was struck speechless with astonishment to see Isabelle beside my bed, letting down her shift. When stark naked she presented one of her bubbies to my lips; she grasped it with one hand and approached it imperiously to my face.

All my passionate love for Isabelle reawakened like lightning, and once more overcome with the foolish desires with which she inspired me I obeyed and sucked the perfect breast, shutting my eyes, intoxicated with joy and happiness.

She did not stir. I could not catch the look of her face because of the dim light from the nightlamp; but I sucked her breast and thought of nothing else.

She drew it away, turned, took my hand and approached it to her buttocks.

I could resist no longer. I jumped out of bed and loaded her with ardent, burning, uninterrupted caresses.

Impassable like a statue, without moving a single muscle, without the least distortion, she suffered herself to be caressed. I lost myself in the raptures of my success, almost wishing to die on the motionless body of this Circe.

I slipped a finger between her thighs and they parted. I titillated her quim and she spread her legs wide. I put my head between them from below and glued my lips to her cunt, while I squeezed her buttocks with both hands.

Intoxicated with my *minettes* I introduced a finger into each orifice and pulled her thighs to my shoulders and bosom. She abandoned herself to whatever I did but did not respond to my foolish caresses.

Fascinated, agitated, and remembering what I had asked Fanny to do, I murmured in a low voice and in a paroxysm of bliss:

"Oh, piddle, piddle into my mouth, and do not be so cold, you, who are usually so hot-natured!"

A tiny jet of urine ran down between my lips, and I swallowed it eagerly; a thin jet, carefully measured out in tiny drops, which enraged me, put me out of sorts, and set my blood on fire.

My mouth enclosed her cunt and did not leave hold of it; my hands fingered her buttocks. She threw herself backwards, her belly projected, setting off her curly-haired mount, her sweet little slit opened its lips and she pressed her hands on my head to prevent me from recovering my senses. She continued to piddle almost drop by drop, and each drop produced the effect of a thousand pricks with a pin, increasing my ardour.

This increased my passion. I was on the point of losing my sense, of going mad; I wanted to escape the fascination, to tear away my lips. Then she squeezed me between her thighs, held my head glued to her cunt, and accelerating her piddling bespattered my neck and breasts with her urine.

She placed herself astride on my head, and a real cataract poured down on my hair and my shoulders.

When she stopped, it oozed down my whole body, and perplexed at this unexpected drenching, I tore off my *chemise*, that it might dry, and got hold of my towel to repair my disordered condition.

She was sitting on my bed and I thought I saw her wicked, sarcastic smile.

I continued to clean myself without paying any attention to her. I resolved to break this rebellious creature. I finished my toilet; and then, giving up my usual gentleness, I pulled her violently by the leg, and whispered: "And now it is your turn. Obey, if you do not wish me to repeat the late correction. I don't mind the noise more than you."

Standing before me she replied: "What's the matter with you! Is it really necessary to fly into a passion when you wish to enjoy sensual pleasure with me? Did I not come on my own account? And have I not consented to whatever you asked?"

"I want the same caresses as I have just bestowed on you."

"Willingly."

"I want to piddle into your mouth."

"Instantly if you like."

She squatted between my thighs, approached her lips to my cunt, took my buttocks in her hands and devoured me with caresses, while she waited for me to piss.

Being more depraved than I, she promised that she reserved me a pleasure I did not know, and she recommended me to follow her impulsion.

"Cease piddling when I touch your bumhole with my finger and turn it to me."

She took in a mouthful of urine, made me turn, and stoop forward or almost lie down before her, then she separated my buttocks, uncovered the orifice, and dexterously squirted in the mouthful she had kept back. It caused me to thrill all over.

Then she took out my chamber pot, saying: "I am not afraid of being inundated, but in order to avoid surprises I think it preferable that you pour out the rest of your pipi in this. I'll rinse my mouth and then we can amuse ourselves in your bed." She became more tractable and I did not insist further; she cuddled herself in my arms.

Then I refound my ardent Isabelle, of whom I was so fond.

"Hear me," whispered she. "Don't be angry if it happens that I insult you or if one of my friends teases you. I cannot help it. It is my nature to be disagreeable to those whom I love, and I love you more than all the others. You can believe me; you can feel it by the shivering of my body united with yours. You cannot imagine how happy I was when you asked me to piddle into your mouth. By that I saw that you were as fond of me as ever.

137

"And while you washed yourself, when you threatened me, I was only afraid that you would be as stupid as before, and that you would not exact the same from me. If you asked, I would drink more than your pipi. When my senses yearn after a person I can gratify the most extravagant fancies. You don't know that I have clutched Lucienne's dildo. We'll fuck one another, if you like."

Belly to belly, bosom to bosom, our tongues billed and cooed in each other's mouth, and by sucking again and again my shoulders and every bit of flesh within her reach the adorable sorceress threatened to bereave me of all my senses. However, I resisted her proposal.

"By deflowering ourselves in secret," replied I, "we risk too much. Let us enjoy what we can do with the lips and leave more violent means alone."

"And if I beseech you to insert it into my bumhole, do you refuse?"

Her tongue cooed and billed at the same time so skillfully in my mouth that I shivered all over and whispered:

"You must decide, my love. Your voluptuousness intoxicates me."

"Oh, then," replied she, "the game is won. Quick, glide towards my bum and prepare it by your caresses."

Oh, the lusciousness of this pleasure. The baggage excelled herself.

Whatever Camille Grandin and all the other worshipers of fat bums say, nothing can be compared to the thousand different resources of Isabelle's delicate arse. It could assume attitudes and poses, it could bound and leap so that the most dispassionate creatures would become all fire and flame. It exulted over my last scruples.

Isabelle tied the famous instrument around my waist, gave me some practical counsels, placed herself between my thighs and I set to work with real adroitness.

It was true! I had my friend. There was not the least doubt.

Between the movements of her back, her catlike contortions, in the midst of her ecstasy she never ceased speaking.

"Oh my sweet Adelina, my own dove, take me, make me your own, spend on me, into my entrails, as I spend under the pressure of your belly. You are my lover, my treasure. I love you and I'll love you for ever. I'll soon devour your lips with my kisses, such kisses as you never received before. Yes, darling, go deeper in, you won't hurt me. On the contrary, I am in Paradise. Your belly burns my buttocks. You love me, do you not? I adore you. A while ago, when I was so cool, I put violence upon myself. I longed to partake of your passion. Stop, stop! Don't move. You are at the bottom. Begin again! Pull out! Oh, I am dying!"

One spasm succeeded another. I inserted the dildo to the root into her beloved arse and my hands fingered it in felicity and only left it to frig her button and nipples. Our lips met.

Sometimes she seized my hand and trembling approached it to her lips to suck all the fingers one after another.

What a night, my Paul! We spent the most part of it together. She only retired when it was dangerous to stay longer. We did not sleep and you should but have seen our faces when we entered the school room next morning.

The most ardent caresses from your sister,

Adelina

V

From the same to the same

We have celebrated the Red Offices and I am actually a member of the confraternity of Red Girls.

It seems like a joke, but it is very serious and I assure you, I shall remember it all my life.

The confraternity consecrates and maintains the sensual customs of the house. The pupils who are considered the most reliable are admitted and it is a kind of freemasonry including former and present pupils, some of their husbands, and the mistresses.

Religion and profanity are combined to interlard the institution. The neophyte who is admitted is looked upon as a girl going to take the veil.

About thirty old pupils, a dozen of whom were accompanied by their husbands, assisted at the Red Offices celebrated in my honour.

As a preparation I withdrew to seclusion with the Red Girls actually at the school for three days. During this retreat I was informed of several ceremonies, to which I must never refuse my concurrence. Likewise I was informed of the importance of the engagements I contracted.

They taught me all kinds of signs by which the Red Brothers and Sisters know each other, as well as propose to one another some pleasure.

I do not mention them here. I hope that you will enter the confraternity some day or other, and then you will learn all about it.

The retreat, during which the greatest continency was observed, in order that we might receive the sacrament in a worthy manner on Sunday morning, exasperated our senses, and the more so, because we all the time got very substantial food.

After communion the guests assembled to take a slight repast and then I was taken to Juliette's to dress as a bride.

From that moment it was only the members of the confraternity that assisted at the ceremonies.

The walls of our little chapel were hung with red velvet; in lieu of the altar, which had been taken away, they had elevated a kind of throne, on which Mrs. Noëmie Breton, a beautiful brunette of twenty-six, was sitting stark naked. She bore the title of chancellor of the confraternity and was married to a very rich jeweller, one of the Brothers.

Clémentine de Burcof and Pauline de Merbef, the two youngest sisters, were sitting, stark naked, too, on a stool on each side.

All the women and girls had put on a severe-looking red dress. They were only severe-looking, for if they fitted tightly round the neck and concealed the figure from head to foot, the skirt was slashed on the right side, so that it could be easily tucked up and was buttoned at long intervals in front and behind; the tippets of the bodices had but to be taken off to exhibit naked breasts, arms, neck and shoulders.

The men wore a red monastic dress.

The assembly sat down in rows, the Misses Géraud in the front rank. A special seat was reserved for me opposite to the chancel; on each side there was a tabouret for my godmothers Nannette and Eve.

The Chaplain appeared in his priestly ornaments, but otherwise stark naked. He was accompanied by two pupils of the middle class officiating as levites.

At the same time the organ set in a symphonic march.

The Chaplain knelt down before Noëmie and his two companions imitated him. He murmured some words in Latin, while the whole congregation was standing.

The march played by the organ ceased and he kissed

141

Noëmie's thighs, rose, tucked up his chasuble and presenting his prick to the levites, who kissed it, he said: "Kiss, my girls, the source of Life and kiss the creative Power."

In the congregation the neighbours kissed each other's lips. Prostrated before Ève and Nannette I kissed the cunt of the former and the buttocks of the latter, which were successively presented me.

The Chaplain approached Noëmie, took her breasts in his hand and sang the following:

> *"God bless thy breast,*
> *God bless thy cunt.*
> *Give luxury*
> *In eternity."*

The organ accompanied him. Then the whole congregation joined, and while feeling the breasts of the women who had taken off their tippets, they sang the next fifteen verses of the hymn.

The Chaplain sang the first line and then the congregation chimed in. He circled round Noëmie, threw himself at her feet, kissed her cunt, rose, and recommenced by taking her breasts into his hands.

The levites executed the same exercise, also the little ones.

When they had finished the hymn there was a minute's silence, after which the Chaplain advanced three steps and cried: "Oh, woman! For the expiation of my sins I throw myself at thy feet and naked as an earthworm I beseech thee to flog me, that I may obtain pardon and mercy."

The levites helped him to strip off his priestly garments and when stark naked he placed himself on all fours on the steps of the chancel opposite to me.

Nannette and Ève took me by the hand and placed me before his posteriors. I knelt down and gave him three sound cuffs after which I kissed his buttocks crosswise, the last kiss in the orifice.

The organ played a gentle, voluptuous march. All the women present advanced one after another to lash him. Before returning to their seats they kissed him as I had done, and afterwards kissed Noëmie's thighs, cunt, and navel.

After their return to their respective seats they tucked up their dresses and received the *feuilles de rose* of the nearest gallant and for want of a man, of the youngest girl in the row.

When everybody had filed off, Noëmie rose, descended the steps of her throne, approached the Chaplain and stripping off the slipper from her right foot, let it wander over the furrow of his arse, while she said: "In the name of my sisters I declare thy sins remitted and I forgive thee."

She straddled over his back turning the wrong way, that is to say, facing the congregation, and laying one hand on his buttocks and rubbing her cunt against his body, she said: "Let Love enter thy soul by my charms and incite thy voluptuousness."

She glided along his whole body from the posteriors to the head; there she rose by degrees, striking up the following hymn:

> *"Hail Priapus,*
> *Hail Coition!*
> *Man and woman*
> *Live and love,*
> *Live and spend!"*

The Chaplain rose in his turn, held out his hand to her and both walked round the nave of the chapel followed by the levites and the two little girls. They continued singing. When passing my chair they bowed to me and then returned to the throne.

Noëmie sat down again, while the Chaplain put on his sacerdotal ornaments and placed himself in his stall with his companions.

This hymn had about twelve verses.

When it was over, four gentlemen went to fetch a charming canopy, quite closed by silver white silk hangings; they approached my seat and shut me up in it with my godmothers.

We were separated from the rest of the congregation.

The men supported the four columns.

The Chaplain commenced singing:

> *"Truth is naked,*
> *And Beauty too!*
> *The Priestess of Love*
> *Who is fond of truth:*
> *Let her body be naked!"*

In proportion as one verse followed another, Nannette and Ève divested me of some of my garments and held them out to be placed on the rail of the chancel.

When I was almost naked Nannette clapped her hands and the organ continued alone the melody of the hymn.

Outside the hangings somebody stamped on the ground, the curtain was drawn and I perceived Noëmie holding out her hand to me.

"Go," said Nannette and Ève.

Though ashamed of my scanty attire I obeyed and accompanied Noëmie to her throne. Making me face the congregation, she took my breasts in her hand and said,

"Look and love! She is a woman by this. May she enter the Temple?"

"She may enter," replied the choir.

Then she turned me round, opened my drawers, gathered up my chemise, exhibited my buttocks and pointing at my bumhole, said:

"Look and love! Men have entered here. Will you accept her in the Temple?"

"We accept her."

She made me turn again, laid bare my belly, placed a finger on my cunt and said.

"Look and love! The altar is closed. Will you honour it in the Temple?"

"We will honour it."

She loosened my stays, took them off and handed them to Pauline; she stripped off my drawers and gave them to Clémentine, then raising my shift to the armpits and asking me to keep it up, she knelt down, kissed my cunt and buttocks, and said: "In the name of the congregation we grant thee admittance to the steps of the Temple! To thy lips we render these caresses and consecrate thy desire to live for our pleasure."

In my turn I stooped before these treasures and paid them my respects.

She sat down on her throne and placed me astride over her thighs, my shift tucked up and my back to her bosom; her hands were clasped over my belly and the tip of her fingers caressed my cunt.

The garments I had just taken off were placed beside the others. The Chaplain took a censer and incensed them while the whole congregation passed and kissed them.

He approached the throne and sent out three to four clouds of smoke. The little girls descended and took hold of his prick, while the choir sang:

> *"Heaven is open*
> *To the elect*
> *Approaching.*
> *The Temple is solemn,*
> *A virgin is sacrificed!"*

He walked round the throne incensing us, then rid

himself of the censer and ascended the steps. As long as they were singing he regaled us both with *minettes*. The little ones did the same to the levites and in the congregation they joined in couples to enjoy the same caresses.

Having finished this he divested me of my boots and stockings and replaced them by a pair of slippers like those worn by all the naked members. Then he led me to the canopy where I found Nannette and Ève in 69.

He began another hymn:

> *"Joy is with us!*
> *Coition is accomplished.*
> *Girls pair off*
> *To all delight."*

The congregation chimed in. He separated Nannette and Ève, who tucked up their skirts; then they took off their tippets. They were imitated by all the other women who henceforth remained "low-necked."

Standing under the canopy I received the *minettes* of my two godmothers and the *feuilles de rose* of the Chaplain.

All the women ranged themselves by twos and walked round the chapel, then they approached the canopy, examined my person, and suffered themselves to be examined from all sides.

They were followed by the men, of whom two carried an iron bedstead, fitted with mattresses and pillows covered by a red velvet drapery, in which they made me lie down.

The curtains of the canopy were drawn and I was alone.

The organ played different tunes. I heard a great noise of footsteps but did not know what was the matter.

A stark naked man entered the canopy. I recognized Dr. Bérnard de Charvey.

He lay down beside me, hugged me in his arms, and

146

kissed and tongued my lips; of course I returned his caresses. The words of the Chaplain officiating near the throne were scarcely audible. However I caught them as well as the answer of the choir.

Judge for yourself! These are the very words of the dialogue, interrupted now and then by a silence of a minute.

"Hail to thee, oh divinity, hail and thanks to thee! Glory be to thy beauty, to thy unconcealed charms."

"Glory be to the arse shining on the throne. Send into ecstasies these wrinkles by the sap of thy lips," replied the choir.

"My tongue penetrates and enjoys the secret way to Heaven. Thy arse is round as the planet Earth. Its hole is the gate of my Heaven."

"Fortune's favours are thine. Thy tongue penetrates into the Temple, the freestones of which seem luminous by the whiteness of the buttocks."

"My tongue titillates the orifice which is all of a twitter. Hark, faithful! The Temple moves. We see it ascend into heaven. Sing praises to it!"

"The Temple be brought down and thy sword touches its entrance. Thou art the Red Girls' anointed. Priest, offer up thy sacrifice!"

Here there was a longer silence than before and a great hubbub in the congregation. The doctor whispered,

"The anointed bumfucks Noëmie and in the Temple every man bumfucks a girl. Even the little ones around with dildoes bumfuck their companions. Your door is open. May I beg my respects to the other and force the entrance?"

He hugged me in his arms. He spoke with his lips close to mine. His belly burnt my belly. The bigness of his prick did not frighten me.

"Yes, force the entrance," replied I. "Deflower me! Let me know all sensual raptures. Oh, my darling! What sufferings and yet what a bliss!"

The contest was long and painful, but interrupted by convulsions carrying off the pain.

In a confusion of voices I heard the following exclamations: "Oh, again! Begin again, yes! Keep me close; hug my arse closer! Yes, yes, again! Go deeper in! Oh, oh, you'll split it! Open your thighs, rub your belly against it! Oh, if it could but get into the hole! Oh, oh! I'm dying!"

At these raving words I jumped in frantic ecstasy. The doctor had begun his attack; I opened my thighs as wide as possible; his tool seemed to tear them as with pincers. He kept me close in his arms; he wanted to break into me and at last he succeeded.

Yes, my dear Paul, your sister is deflowered. At this moment she knows all about love. I never though it possible that I could take in such a big lump of flesh between my thighs. Yet the doctor's prick disappeared entirely within me.

However, I must confess that he had moistened my cunt with different ingredients and that he had put plenty of cold cream on his prick.

Add to this that my skillfully maintained excitement had predisposed me for otherwise violent pain. I do not think that even martyrdom would have frightened me.

In the most perfect ecstasy, twisted together so that our bodies were but one, we awaited the moment when it would be calm outside.

Then the doctor kissed my eyes, nose, cheeks, ears, lips, and nipples, rose and clapped his hands. Nannette and Ève appeared, bringing me all that was necessary for my toilet, and the choir began a new hymn.

"The virgin has surrendered
Glory be to Nature!
Love, the immortal
Will favour her faithful."

When I had finished my toilet the canopy was removed. My godmothers took me by the hand and we went the round of the chapel, after which I was placed on a choir opposite to the throne.

My clothes were no longer on the rail of the chancel and I was just asking myself whether I had to remain stark naked, when the Chaplain, the levites, Clémentine, and Pauline, whom I had not seen, came from the sacristy with different garments. The organ played some modulations and the choir sang:

"Array the neophyte
In her festival attire
Her Sisters expect her,
She reigns with them!"

During this hymn the Chaplain first threw himself at my feet and kissed my whole body. Then he rose and passed a red tulle jacket over my head. It but just came down to my navel. He added two petticoats, the skirt, the bodice, the tippet, the stockings and shoes—a complete red attire.

The canoness rose and extended her hand over my head. Great silence.

"Red Girl," said she. "From this moment and till your dying day, whenever you are called, you belong to the members of the confraternity and to the rules with which you are made acquainted. Do you consent?"

"I consent."

"You may depend on our protection everywhere; but you too must promise to protect our people everywhere.

Your soul, your heart, your senses are forever united with all of us. Do you accept?"

"I accept."

Then we kissed each other tenderly, and a general handplay began, interrupted by other caresses, sucking, licking, downfalls, fucking, and spending.

But what a state you must be in, my dear Paul, on reading all this! Your blood is on fire, and you long for the pleasures which were so churlishly interrupted. You did not find the Gates of Heaven open, as I did. Oh, if our parents would but place you at a college in Paris, we should see each other often and often. You may be sure of the sympathy of the Misses Géraud and Ève.

The holidays approach. Shall we meet? And if we meet, shall I find an opportunity of initiating you into my science, of inculcating it in you by luscious filthiness? Wish for it! I am ready for anything and shall afterwards introduce you to all my friends of the congregation.

Good gracious, what extravagant meetings! Good bye, darling, millions and millions of suckings and tonguings, wherever you want to feel my lips. Yes, Paul, I shall let you fuck me, you shall put your strong young prick deep into your loving sister's cunt and spend till you can spend no more. We first learnt the rudiments of love together, my dear Paul, and now you shall learn the essence of a sister's love by using your throbbing prick to draw forth the essence from your sister's longing cunt. *Adieu.*

Your sister,

Adelina

Order These Selected Blue Moon Titles

Souvenirs From a Boarding School $7.95	Shades of Singapore $7.95
The Captive $7.95	Images of Ironwood $7.95
Ironwood Revisited $7.95	What Love $7.95
Sundancer $7.95	Sabine $7.95
Julia $7.95	An English Education $7.95
The Captive II $7.95	The Encounter $7.95
Shadow Lane $7.95	Tutor's Bride $7.95
Belle Sauvage $7.95	A Brief Education $7.95
Shadow Lane III $7.95	Love Lessons $7.95
My Secret Life $9.95	Shogun's Agent $7.95
Our Scene $7.95	The Sign of the Scorpion $7.95
Chrysanthemum, Rose & the Samurai $7.95	Women of Gion $7.95
Captive V $7.95	Mariska I $7.95
Bombay Bound $7.95	Secret Talents $7.95
Sadopaideia $7.95	Beatrice $7.95
The New Story of O $7.95	S&M: The Last Taboo $8.95
Shadow Lane IV $7.95	"Frank" & I $7.95
Beauty in the Birch $7.95	Lament $7.95
Laura $7.95	The Boudoir $7.95
The Reckoning $7.95	The Bitch Witch $7.95
Ironwood Continued $7.95	Story of O $5.95
In a Mist $7.95	Romance of Lust $9.95
The Prussian Girls $7.95	Ironwood $7.95
Blue Velvet $7.95	Virtue's Rewards $5.95
Shadow Lane V $7.95	The Correct Sadist $7.95
Deep South $7.95	The New Olympia Reader $15.95

Visit our website at www.bluemoonbooks.com

ORDER FORM
Attach a separate sheet for additional titles.

Title   Quantity   Price

_____   ____   _____

_____   ____   _____

_____   ____   _____

_____   ____   _____

                     Shipping and Handling (see charges below)   _____

                                  Sales tax (in CA and NY)   _____

                                                Total   _____

Name _____

Address _____

City _____ State _____ Zip _____

Daytime telephone number _____

❑ Check   ❑ Money Order   (US dollars only. No COD orders accepted.)

Credit Card # _____ Exp. Date _____

❑ MC   ❑ VISA   ❑ AMEX

Signature _____
                     (if paying with a credit card you must sign this form.)

Shipping and Handling charges:*

Domestic: $4 for 1st book, $.75 each additional book. International: $5 for 1st book, $1 each additional book
*rates in effect at time of publication. Subject to Change.

Mail order to Publishers Group West, Attention: Order Dept., 1700 Fourth St., Berkeley, CA 94710,
or fax to (510) 528-3444.

PLEASE ALLOW 4-6 WEEKS FOR DELIVERY. ALL ORDERS SHIP VIA 4TH CLASS MAIL.

Look for Blue Moon Books at your favorite local bookseller
or from your favorite online bookseller.